The Heart of the Ancient Wood

The Heart of the Ancient Wood

Charles G. D. Roberts

Introduction by Joseph Gold
General Editor: Malcolm Ross

New Canadian Library No. 110

McClelland and Stewart Limited

0-7710-9210-5

This book was originally published in 1900 in the United States of America by J. B. Lippincott Company and in Great Britain by Silver, Burdett & Company.

The Canadian Publishers
McClelland and Stewart Limited
25 Hollinger Road, Toronto

Printed and bound in Canada

Contents

To
L. W. v. U.

Introduction

It is tempting to begin an introduction to Roberts' extraordinary fable by saying that it could hardly be more Canadian, could not more accurately represent the sort of myth we love to play a rôle in when we are abroad. A girl and her friendship with a great black bear, a bear that she brings home and feeds honey at the table like some great uncivilized Winnie the Pooh? Why of course, didn't you know – it happens all the time back home! Tempting, and in some fragmentary way true, as myths about ourselves must have truth and as bears do have a special and privileged place in our culture. But this would hardly suggest that Roberts is here writing serious or lasting fiction, worthy of reprinting, of study, of our earnest and expectant attention and I would like to persuade those who do not know this book that this is precisely what he is doing. Roberts may never acquire the reputation of a major Canadian novelist, and will probably remain, as he is now, ranked among our foremost poets, but I believe he is in the forefront of men of letters who will be recognized increasingly as important in helping us to understand ourselves, and in creating apprehensible images of our culture. This is not to deny that Roberts is a highly polished and sophisticated writer, capable of extraordinary feats of description and natural detail, of perspective and lyricism or to claim that he cannot write fiction symbolic and intricate enough to satisfy even the most demanding Ph.D. student, hungry for a topic. It is simply that, when all is said and done, Roberts will be important for tackling themes that matter essentially to our culture and in a way that is unique in Canadian writing.

In this novel Roberts attempts to write of universal forces, love, innocence, exile, death, and the impact on such human experience of the local, wild, frontier of eastern New Brunswick, which is the Canada he knows. He does this by creating a fable and then transcends it by symbolically rendering his materials into a genuine Canadian myth. None of this is wholly successful but the result is so compelling and so odd, indeed, that it deserves our attention and is certain to engross and entertain us. *The Heart of the Ancient Wood* is an ambitious novel. It tells the romantic tale of a young, fatherless girl, growing up in the wilderness and discovering her own womanhood and humanity. It presents a moral fable of man's encounter with untamed nature, and the conflicts and harmonies possible in such a meeting. And it weaves into this an allegory of the relations between the sexes.

There are two obvious primary influences on this novel, and distinct elements of these are traceable throughout. Both Hawthorne's *Scarlet Letter* and Shakespeare's *Tempest* present images of an exile by means of which the protagonists achieve new assessments of their own humanity. In each case these "aliens" are cast out from the community and meet the new and strange world of nature. In these "New World" settings they are thrown upon their own resources and perceptions and because they are human, they build new communities, only now the communities rest on stronger foundations. This, at least, is the ideal to which these fictions aspire. The sources of their humanity have been examined and tested personally, in actual trial, and the assumptions of the larger community have been distanced and put to the test. A return to civilization is in the form of a renewal of contract, of covenant, via a new birth so to speak, a kind of adult baptism in which the newly discovered old truths have been achieved at great cost and then internalized forever. The residence abroad has been precisely paralleled by spiritual quest. Shakespeare's Miranda cannot be denied her human impulse to rejoin the community of men and cannot help but find Ferdinand the most beautiful creature in her island, just as Roberts' Miranda cannot resist her attraction to Dave, who suddenly appears in her "clearing" and is finally chosen over all the other creatures, even over Krook, the bear, whom Miranda finally sacrifices. Both Mirandas are able to see the men they discover as superior animals, thus providing the reader with a fresh perception of man in nature, unadorned man, glimpsed for just a moment without all the assumptions that cloud our normal vision.

Hester Prynne is cast out of the community by a people that has drawn too sharp a line between its own human codes and the primitive wilderness which surrounds it. To deny those links between the primitive and the civilized is to fragment their humanity; their absoluteness is ruthless, as unrelenting, ironically enough, as the hunting and killing of the wild creatures whom they have relegated to the devil's domain. Hester has been guilty of adultery and Pearl, the offspring of this illicit union, has the marks of a not-quite-human being. While Roberts, like the good Anglican of 1900 that he was and conscious of his readers' delicacy, cannot make his Kirstie an out-and-out adulteress, he skirts all round and very near that title and even suggests that the gossips of the settlement think of her as having sinned exactly as Hester did. Miranda is Pearl's counterpart, the daughter of a deserted and persecuted mother and the two of them leave the hostile community, "where a shallow spite, sharpened by her proud reticence and supplied with arrows of injury by her misfortunes, made life an undesisting and immitigable hurt to her," (pp. 32-33) for the peace of the forest, preferring genuine exile to the civilized isolation and the acrimony of their neighbours. The sylph-like child of this new wilderness home is called the "great-eyed and fairy-like Miranda" and is gifted with a penetrating vision that can pierce the secrets of the wild. Both mother and daughter wear scarlet symbols which, like the letter A on Hester's breast, is an indispensable part of their clothing, though for less obvious reasons.

> Nevertheless the vein of contradiction which streaked her baby heart with bright inconsistencies bade her demand always a bit of scarlet ribbon about her neck. This whim Kirstie humoured with a smile, recognizing in it a perpetuation of the scarlet kerchief about her own black hair. (pp. 48-49)

Roberts persists in reminding us of these wayward impulses a hundred pages later.

> The scarlet ribbon which Miranda the woman, like Miranda the child, wore always about her neck, seemed in her the symbol of an ineradicable strangeness of spirit, while Kirstie's scarlet kerchief expressed but the passion which burned perennial beneath its wearer's quietude. (p. 148)

Doubtless, Roberts means to suggest by this some human, carnal link with the whims of a human kin as opposed to an animal world, for we are told often that it is this scarlet ribbon that most fascinates and confuses the animals.

While Hawthorne and Shakespeare seem, at least to me, obvious influences on *The Heart of the Ancient Wood*, two much later works contain elements similar enough to throw further light on Roberts' work, continuing, as it were, a tradition of the quest-in-the-wilderness theme. Conrad's *Heart of Darkness* should be mentioned in passing, not only because its title teaches us that Roberts also did not mean only "depths" by his use of "heart." He means, as Conrad later meant, the very essence and being and balance, the poise, the beat, the life of the ancient human genesis, to which Miranda must draw close before she can discover what she is, how she differs from the wild creatures and what she wants. Conrad isolates and heightens that symbolic element of quest which is woven more lightly and less carefully through Roberts' novel. But Roberts, too, makes much of Old Dave's long journey through the woods to the clearing which he will ready for the exiles' residence, watched as he is all the way by the creatures of the trails, the woods' native inhabitants who signal to each other the presence of the alien. The author is anxious to suggest that this place is more than a nearby suburb of the settlement. It is far off and to be reached only by the initiated and to be inhabited only by the stouthearted.

> As she emerged from the twilight and came out upon the sunny bleakness of the clearing, the unspeakable loneliness of it struck a sudden pallor into her grave dark face. For a moment, even the humanity that was hostile to her seemed less cruel than this voiceless solitude. Then her resolution came back. (p. 33)

The other much more recent work that recalls for me this Roberts' novel and which also creates an animal fable in which a boy learns of his links with man by an initiation into the wilderness, is Faulkner's *The Bear.* I believe that Faulkner would have thoroughly enjoyed *The Heart of the Ancient Wood*, seeing in it, in spite of its weaknesses, the powerful grasp of mythic forces at work, the profound respect for the natural, and the search for definition of the human place in a world in which we are too often the brutal guests rather than the graceful inhabitants by right. Roberts in his turn would have honoured the beauty and the themes of *The Bear.* There he would have discovered Ben instead of Krook, and in him he would have recognized the same giant, legendary bear, bigger than any ever seen in the area, ruler of the forest, the "Big Woods" in one case, the "Ancient Wood" in the other. Both bears are almost magical in their knowledge and ancient wisdom, both bears are part of the ritual initiation of their respective children acolytes, Miranda and Isaac, and both bears are killed, not in the normal hunt, but at close quarters in a sacrificial and symbolic slaughter, witnessing and signifying an end to innocence.

I have made these references to influences and parallels in order to provide some kind of perspective on this unusual novel to indicate that as we read we are seeing a tradition at work and that the themes that Roberts undertakes are not merely far-fetched tales of wildlife adventure but profound suggestions as to what is involved in being human in a human society. Beyond this tradition, beyond the recurrent myths and the familiar fables, Roberts has presented some issues uniquely his own and in some ways uniquely Canadian. They are also curiously modern, these issues, indeed I think far ahead of their time and of immediate significance to us. *The Heart of the Ancient Wood* is a moral fable, presenting unusual and even unlikely events, in which animals and human beings interact in a story that becomes allegorical. Miranda, the fatherless exile-child, is only partially human and her closest companion is a bear, a kind of second mother to her, who initiates her into all the wilderness ways and is in her turn partly domesticated, even taking some of her meals in the house and losing some of her fear of human beings, becoming in fact partly human as Miranda becomes partly wild.

Into this scene emerges young Dave, a trapper and woodsman, who is largely insensitive to the wild creatures, making little or no identification with them, and seeing animals only as bearing valuable pelts and edible carcasses. A triangle is thus formed in which Miranda becomes the arena of conflict, torn between her wild allegiances and her human and sexual needs and compulsions. The triangle is finally resolved by Miranda saving the man's life by shooting the bear, using the rifle which she has always abhorred. It is a simple and even naive story but in telling it, Roberts has revealed some interesting things. Miranda has had to learn that she is an animal and that animals kill each other. She must confront her kinship with both sides of nature. The savagery of nature surrounds her yet her view has been selective and partially blind. In order to be fully human and thus fully herself she must first come to terms with her animal nature, and this includes her sexual response to Dave, ever so subtly hinted at by Roberts. This realization must be whole, encompassing not only the cubs and kittens she so loves, the teddy-bear quality of Krook which is the side revealed to her, but also the red of tooth and claw exposed inescapably at last when Krook is intent on rending Dave to pieces. Miranda's vegetarianism has not extended to fish, which she has hardly regarded as animal at all, nor does she have any compassion for the wolves, which she sees as savagely dangerous and beyond her sympathies as they threaten her other friends. These inconsistencies are there to sow the seeds from which will grow the destruction of her partial and sentimental primitivism. While Miranda sees herself as having entire kinship with a false version of the wild, Dave is conscious of no kinship whatever with his equally false version. Her humanization involves a loss of innocence that is largely ignorance, while his humanization involves acquiring an innocence that necessitates an awakening of his imagination. He develops new sympathies for the wild and greater respect for its mysteries through Miranda's tutelage and while she learns that kindness and cruelty, love and hate, desire and repulsion are part of a single, intricate whole, he agrees to forego his profession and turn to surveying lumber. Out of their mutual influences Roberts tries to convey to the reader the necessity for the unsentimentalized, realistic respect for the wilderness that he finds essential to genuinely humane survival in the Canadian encounter with the vast ancient wood that the settlers found here. Based on thorough knowledge, there must be love and admiration and humility, even from those who hunt and kill. Roberts conveys his own such respect in many superb passages of which the following is perhaps the finest:

> Miranda had learned many things already from her year among the folk of the wood. One of these things was that all the furtive folk dreaded and resented rough movement. Their

> manners were always beyond reproach. The fiercest of them moved ever with an aristocratic grace and poise. They knew the difference between swiftness and haste. All abruptness they abhorred. In lines of beauty they eluded their enemies. They killed in curves. (p. 111)

There are many weaknesses in the presentation of this fable for our times. The courtship of Dave and Miranda and their shifts in perception are much too hurried and illustrated by rather obvious, symbolic landmarks. There is not much consistency in Dave's giving up hunting, only to lend himself to the destruction of the forest itself and one cannot help but feel a sense of his loss of manhood in making an alteration in his life that will in reality alter nothing. The dialogue between people is, as always in Roberts, the weakest part of the book and all the many themes I have cited are woven together hurriedly and uncomfortably so that the whole fabric is coarse finally, rather than smooth. Nevertheless, Roberts has attempted an encounter here with issues of major significance, namely the meaning, consequences and possibilities in man's encounter with ecology, as it was found in Canada nearly a century ago. Perhaps after all these are *the* issues. The balance, the poise, the grace and economy of nature require our humblest responses, not merely for our physical but for our spiritual survival. Perhaps Roberts saw that this was the last frontier, this Canada the last possibility, and that long after his novel had been a popular story these would be the concerns that would cry for attention. Perhaps Roberts felt in a peculiarly Canadian way, as Thoreau felt in a peculiarly American way, that here was a last, critical, priceless chance, a moment in history when man, poised before the last great, unpolluted, unspoilt wilderness on his planet, might gaze with sufficient awe and wonder on his new but ancient world and find from somewhere the imagination, the wit, the humour, love and respect to blend somehow his own estranged heart with that of the ancient wood, become indeed a part of that ecology that breathes out of Roberts' work. It is my view that from his glimpse of such possibilities and from his own intense fascination with his beloved New Brunswick woods, Roberts created one of the most provocative of our early novels, now reprinted here. It is a work that cannot but intrigue a careful and sensitive reader.

Joseph Gold
University of Waterloo

The Heart of the Ancient Wood

THE HEART OF THE ANCIENT WOOD

Chapter I

The Watchers of the Trail

NOT indolently soft, like that which sifts in green shadow through the leafage of a summer garden, but tense, alertly and mysteriously expectant, was the silence of the forest. It was somehow like a vast bubble of glass, blown to a fineness so tenuous that a small sound, were it but to strike the one preordained and mystic note, might shatter it down in loud ruin. Yet it had existed there flawless for generations, transmuting into its own quality all such infrequent and inconsequent disturbance as might arise from the far-off cry of the panther, or the thin chirp of the clambering nuthatch, the long, solemn calling of the taciturn moose, twice or thrice repeated under the round October moon, or the noise of some great wind roaring heavily in the remote tops of pine and birch and hemlock. Few and slender were the rays of sun that pierced down through those high tops. The air that washed the endless vistas of brown-green shadow was of a marvellous clarity, not blurred by any stain of dust or vapour. Its magical transparency was confusing to an eye not born and bred to it, making the far branches seem near, and the near twigs unreal, disturbing the accustomed perspective, and hinting of some elvish deception in familiar and apparent things.

The trail through the forest was rough and long unused. In spots the mosses and ground vines had so overgrown it that only the broad scars on the tree trunks, where the lumberman's axe had blazed them for a sign, served to distinguish it from a score of radiating vistas. But just here, where it climbed a long, gradual slope, the run of water down its slight hollow had sufficed to keep its worn stones partly bare. Moreover, though the furrowing steps of man had left it these many seasons untrodden, it was never wholly neglected. A path once fairly differentiated by the successive passings of feet will keep, almost forever, a spell for the persuasion of all that go afoot. The old trail served the flat, shuffling tread of Kroof, the great she-bear, as she led her half-grown cub to feast on the blueberry patches far up the mountain. It caught the whim of Ten-Tine, the caribou, as he convoyed his slim cows down to occasional pasturage in the alder swamps of the slow Quah-Davic.

On this September afternoon, when the stillness seemed to wait wide-eyed, suddenly a cock-partridge came whirring up the trail, alighted on a gnarled limb, turned his outstretched head twice from side to side as he peered with his round beads of eyes, and then stiffened into the moveless semblance of one of the fungoid excrescences with which the tree was studded. A moment more and the sound of footsteps, of the nails of heavy boots striking on the stones, grew conspicuous against the silence. Up the trail came slouching, with a strong but laborious stride, a large, grizzled man in grey homespuns. His trousers were stuffed unevenly into the tops of his rusty boots; on his head was a drooping, much-battered hat of a felt that had been brown; from his belt hung a large knife in a fur-fringed leather sheath; and over his shoulder he carried an axe, from the head of which swung a large bundle. The bundle was tied up in a soiled patchwork quilt of gaudy colours, and from time to time there came from it a flat clatter suggestive of tins. At one side protruded the black handle of a frying-pan, half wrapped up in newspaper.

Had he been hunter or trapper, Dave Titus would have carried a gun. Or had he been a townsman, a villager, or even an ordinary small country farmer, he would have taken care to be well armed before penetrating a day's journey into the heart of the ancient wood. But being a lumberman, he was neither quite of the forest nor quite of the open. His winters he spent in the very deep of the wilderness, in a log camp crowded with his mates, eating salt pork, beans, hot bread; and too busy all day long with his unwearying axe to wage any war upon the furred and feathered people. His summers were passed with plough and hoe on a little half-tilled farm in the Settlements. He had, therefore, neither the desire to kill nor the impulse to fear, as he traversed, neutral and indifferent, these silent but not desolated territories. Not desolated; for the ancient wood was populous in its reserve. Observant, keen of vision, skilled in woodcraft though he was, the grave-faced old lumberman saw nothing in the tranquillity about him save tree trunks, and fallen, rotting remnants, and mossed hillocks, and thickets of tangled shrub. He noted the difference, not known to the general eye, between white spruce, black spruce, and fir, between grey birch and yellow birch, between withe-wood and viburnum; and he read instinctively, by the lichen growth about their edges, how many seasons had laid their disfeaturing touch upon those old scars of the axe which marked the trail. But for all his craft he thought himself alone. He guessed not of the many eyes that watched him.

In truth, his progress was the focus of an innumerable attention. The furtive eyes that followed his movements were some of them timorously hostile, some impotently vindictive, some indifferent; but all alien. All were at one in the will to remain unseen; so all kept an unwinking immobility, and were swallowed up, as it were, in the universal stillness.

The cock-partridge, a well-travelled bird who knew the Settlements and their violent perils, watched with indignant apprehension. Not without purpose had he come whirring so tumultuously up the trail, a warning to the ears of all the wood-folk. His fear was lest the coming of this grey man-figure should mean an invasion of those long, black sticks which went off with smoky bang when they were pointed. He effaced himself till his brown mottled feathers were fairly one with the mottled brown bark of his perch; but his liquid eyes lost not a least movement of the stranger.

The nuthatch, who had been walking straight up the perpendicular trunk of a pine when the sound of the alien footsteps froze him, peered fixedly around the tree. His eye, a black point of inquiry, had never before seen anything like this clumsy and slow-moving shape, but knew it for something dangerous. His little slaty head, jutting at an acute angle from the bark, looked like a mere caprice of knot or wood fungus; but it had the singular quality of moving smoothly around the trunk, as the lumberman advanced, so as to keep him always in view.

Equally curious, but quivering with fear, two wood-mice watched him intently, sitting under the broad leaf of a skunk-cabbage not three feet from the trail. Their whiskers touched each other's noses, conveying thrills and palpitations of terror as he drew near, drew nearer, came — and passed. But not unless that blind, unheeding heel had been on the very point of crushing them would they have disobeyed the prime law of their tribe, which taught them that to sit still was to sit unseen.

A little farther back from the trail, under a spreading tangle of ironwood, on a bed of tawny moss crouched a hare. His ears lay quite flat along his back. His eyes watched with aversion, not unmixed with scorn, the heavy, tall creature that moved with such effort and such noise. "Never," thought the hare, disdainfully, "would he be able to escape from his enemies!" As the delicate current of air which pulses imperceptibly through the forest bore the scent of the man to the hare's hiding-place, the fine nostrils of the latter worked rapidly with dislike. On a sudden, however, came a waft of other scent; and the hare's form seemed to shrink to half its size, the nostrils rigidly dilating.

It was the scent of the weasel — to the hare it was the very essence of death. But it passed in an instant, and then the hare's exact vision saw whence it came. For the weasel, unlike all the other folk of the wood, was moving. He was keeping pace with the man, at a distance of some ten feet from the trail. So fitted, however, was his colouring to his surrounding, so shadow-like in its soundless grace was his motion, that the man never discerned him. The weasel's eyes were fixed upon the intruder with a malignancy of hate that might well have seared through his unconsciousness. Fortunately for the big lumberman, the weasel's strength, stupendous for its size, was in no way commensurate with its malice; or the journey would have come to an end just there, and the gaudy bundle would have rested on the trail to be a long wonder to the mice.

The weasel presently crossed the yet warm scent of a mink, whereupon he threw up his vain tracking of the woodman and turned off in disgust. He did not like the mink, and wondered what that fish-eater could be wanting so far back from the water. He was not afraid exactly,— few animals know fear so little as the weasel, — but he kept a small shred of prudence in his savage little heart, and he knew that the mink was scarcely less ferocious than himself, while nearly thrice his size.

From the mossy crotch of an old ash tree, slanting over the trail, a pair of pale, yellow-green eyes, with fine black slits for pupils, watched the traveller's march. They were set in a round, furry head, which was pressed flat to the branch and partly overhung it. The pointed, tufted ears lay flat back upon the round brown head. Into the bark of the branch four sets of razor-edged claws dug themselves venomously; for the wild-cat knew, perhaps through some occult communication from its far-off domesticated kin of hearth and door-sill, that in man he saw the one unvanquishable enemy to all the folk of the wood. He itched fiercely to drop upon the man's bowed neck, just where it showed, red and defenceless, between the gaudy bundle and the rim of the brown hat. But the wild-cat, the lesser lynx, was heir to a ferocity well tempered with discretion, and the old lumberman slouched onward unharmed, all ignorant of that green gleam of hate playing upon his neck.

It was a very different gaze which followed him from the heart of a little colony of rotting stumps, in a dark hollow near the trail. Here, in the cool gloom, sat Kroof, the bear, rocking her huge body contemplatively from side to side on her haunches, and occasionally slapping off a mosquito from the sensitive tip of her nose. She had no cub running with her that season, to keep her busy and anxious. For an hour she had been comfortably rocking, untroubled by fear or desire or indignation; but when the whirring of the cock-partridge gave her warning, and the grating of the nailed boots caught her ear, she had stiffened instantly into one of the big brown stumps. Her little red eyes followed the stranger with something like a twinkle in them. She had seen men before, and she neither actively feared them nor actively disliked them. Only, averse to needless trouble, she cared not to intrude herself on their notice; and therefore she obeyed the custom of the wood, and kept still. But the bear is far the most human of all the furry wood-folk, the most versatile and largely tolerant, the least enslaved by its surroundings. It has an ample sense of humour, also, that most humane of gifts; and it was with a certain relish that Kroof recognized in the grey-clad stranger one of those loud axemen from whose camp, far down by the Quah-Davic, she had only last winter stolen certain comforting rations of pork. Her impulse was to rock again with satisfaction at the thought, but that would have been out of keeping with her present character as a decaying stump, and she restrained herself. She also restrained a whimsical impulse to knock the gaudy bundle from the stranger's back with one sweep of her great paw, and see if it might not contain many curious and edifying things, if not even pork. It was not till she had watched him well up the trail and fairly over the crest of the slope that, with a deep, non-committal grunt, she again turned her attention to the mosquitoes, which had been learning all the tenderness of a bear's nose.

These were but a few of the watchers of the trail, whose eyes, themselves unseen, scrutinized the invader of the ancient wood. Each step of all his journey was well noted. Not so securely and unconsideringly would he have gone, however, had he known that only the year before there had come a pair of panthers to occupy a vacant lair on the neighbouring mountain side. No, his axe would have swung free, and his eyes would have scanned searchingly every overhanging branch; for none knew better than old Dave Titus how dangerous a foe was the tawny northern panther. But just now, as it chanced, the panther pair were hunting away over in the other valley, the low, dense-wooded valley of the Quah-Davic.

As matters stood, for all the watchers that marked him, the old lumberman walked amid no more imminent menace than that which glittered down upon him from four pairs of small bright eyes, high up among the forking limbs of an old pine. In a well-hidden hole, as in a nursery window, were bunched the smooth heads of four young squirrels, interested beyond measure in the strange animal plodding so heavily below them. Had they been Settlement squirrels they would, without doubt, have passed shrill comments, more or less uncomplimentary; for the squirrel loves free speech. But when he dwells among the folk of the ancient wood he, even he, learns reticence; and, in that neighbourhood, if a young squirrel talks out loud in the nest, the consequences which follow have a tendency to be final. When the old lumberman had passed out of their range of view, the four little heads disappeared into the musky brown depths of the nest, and talked the event over in the smallest of whispers.

As the lumberman journeyed, covering good ground with his long, slouching stride, the trail gradually descended through a tract where moss-grown boulders were strown thick among the trees. Presently the clear green brown of the mid-forest twilight took a pallor ahead of him, and the air began to lose its pungency of bark and mould. Then came the flat, soft smell of sedge; and the trees fell away; and the traveller came out upon the shores of a lake. Its waters were outspread pearly-white from a fringe of pale green rushes, and the opposite shore looked black against the pale, hazy sky. A stone's throw beyond the sedge rose a little naked island of black rock, and in the sheen of water off its extremity there floated the black, solitary figure of a loon.

As the lumberman came out clear of the trees, and the gaudy colours of his bundle caught its eye, the bird sank itself lower in the water till only its erect neck and wedge-shaped head were in view. Then, opening wide its beak, it sent forth its wild peal of inexplicable and disconcerting laughter — an affront to the silence, but a note of monition to all the creatures of the lake. The loon had seen men before, and despised them, and found pleasure in proclaiming the scorn. It despised even the long, black sticks that went off with smoky bang when pointed; for had it not learned, in another lake near the Settlement, to dive at the flash and so elude the futile, spattering pellets that flew from the stick.

The lumberman gave neither a first nor a second thought to the loon at all, but quickened his pace in the cheerful open. The trail now led some way along the lake-side, till the shore became higher and rougher, and behind a cape of rock a bustling river emptied itself, carrying lines of foam and long ripples far out across the lake's placidity. From the cape of rock towered a bleak, storm-whitened rampike, which had been a pine tree before the lightning smote it. Its broken top was just now serving as the perch of a white-headed eagle. The great bird bent fierce yellow eyes upon the stranger, — eyes with a cruel-looking, straight overhang of brow,—and stretched its flat-crowned, snake-like head far out to regard him. It opened the rending sickle of its beak and yelped at him — three times at deliberated interval. Then the traveller vanished again into the gloom of the wood, and the arrogant bird plumed himself upon a triumph.

The trail now touched the river, only to forsake it and plunge into the heart of a growth of young Canada balsam. This sweet-smelling region traversed, the soft roar of the stream was left behind, and the forest resumed its former monumental features. For another hour the man tramped steadily, growing more conscious of his load, more and more uninterested in his surroundings; and for another hour his every step was noted by intent, unwinking eyes from branch and thicket. Then again the woods fell apart with a spreading of daylight. He came out upon the spacious solitude of a clearing; pushed through the harsh belt of blackberry and raspberry canes, which grew as a neutral zone between forest and open; picked his way between the burned stumps and crimson fireweeds of a long desolate pasture; and threw down his bundle at the door of the loneliest cabin he had ever chanced to see.

Chapter II

The Cabin in the Clearing

THOUGH a spur of black, uncompromising spruce woods gave it near shelter on the north, the harshly naked clearing fell away from it on the other three sides, and left the cabin bleak. Not a shrub nor a sapling broke the bareness of the massive log walls, whence the peeling bark hung in strips that fluttered desolately to every wind. Only a few tall and ragged weeds, pale green, and with sparse, whitish grey seed-heads, straggled against the foundation logs. The rough deal door sagged on its hinges, half open. The door-sill gaped with a wide crack, rotted along the edges; and along the crack grew a little fringe of grass, ruthlessly crushed down by old Dave's gaudy bundle. The two small windows still held fragments of glass in their sashes, — glass thick with spiders' webs, and captive dust, and the *débris* of withered insects. The wide-eaved roof, well built of split cedar-slabs, with a double overlay of bark, seemed to have turned a brave front to the assault of the seasons, and showed few casualties. Some thirty paces to one side stood another cabin, lower and more roughly built, whose roof had partly fallen in. This had been the barn, — this, with a battered lean-to of poles and interwoven spruce boughs against its southerly wall. The barn was set down at haphazard, in no calculated or contenting relation to the main building, but just as the lay of the hillocks had made it simplest to find a level for the foundations. All about it grew a tall, coarse grass, now grey and drily rustling, the brood of seeds which in past years had sifted through the chinks from the hay stored in the loft. The space between the two buildings, and for many square yards about the cabin door, was strewn thick with decaying chips, through which the dock and plantain leaves, hardy strangers from the Settlement, pushed up their broad, obtuse intrusion. Over toward the barn lay the bleached skeleton of a bob-sled, the rusted iron shoe partly twisted from one runner; and in the centre of the space, where the chips gathered thickest and the plantains had gained least ground, lay a split chopping-log, whose scars bore witness to the vigour of a vanished axe.

The old lumberman fetched a deep breath, depressed by the immeasurable desolation. His eye wandered over the weedy fields, long fallow, and the rugged stump lots aflame here and there with patches of golden-rod and crimson fire-weed. To him these misplaced flares of colour seemed only to make the loneliness more forlorn, perhaps by their association with homelier and kindlier scenes. He leaned on his axe, and pointed indefinitely with his thumb.

"Squat here! an' farm yon!" said he, with contemplative disapproval. "I'd see myself furder first! But Kirstie Craig's got grit for ten men!"

Then he pushed the door open, lifting it to ease the hinge, and stepped peeringly inside. As he did so, a barn-swallow flickered out through a broken pane.

The cabin contained two rooms, one much smaller than the other. The ceiling of the smaller room was formed by a loft at the level of the eaves, open toward the main room, which had no ceiling but the roof of slabs and bark. Here, running up through the east gable, was a chimney of rough stone, arched at the base to contain a roomy hearth, with swinging crane and rusted andirons. A settle of plank was fixed along the wall under the window. Down the middle of the room, its flank toward the hearth, ran a narrow table of two planks, supported by unsmoothed stakes driven into the floor. In the corner farthest from the chimney, over against the partition, was a shallow sleeping bunk, a mere oblong box partly filled with dry red pickings of spruce and hemlock. The floor was littered with dead leaves and with ashes wind-drifted from the hearth.

Old Dave went over and glanced into the bunk. He found the spruce pickings scratched up toward one end, and arranged as they would be for no human occupant.

"Critters been sleepin' here!" he muttered. Then laying down his bundle, he turned his attention to the hearth, and soon the old chimney tasted once more, after its long solitude, the cheer of the familiar heat.

It was now close upon sundown, and the lumberman was hungry. He untied the grimy, many-coloured quilt. Kroof, the she-bear, had been right in her surmise as to that bundle. It did contain pork, — a small, well-salted chunk of it; and presently the red-and-white-streaked slices were sputtering crisply in the pan, while the walls and roof saturated themselves once more in old-remembered savours.

By the time the woodman had made his meal of fried pork and bread, and had smoked out his little pipe of blackened clay, a lonely twilight had settled about the cabin in the clearing. He went to the door and looked out. A white mist, rising along the forest edges, seemed to cut him off from all the world of men; and a few large stars, at vast intervals, came out solemnly upon the round of sky. He shut the door, dropped the wooden latch into its slot, and threw a dry sliver upon the hearth to give him light for turning in. He was sparing of the firewood, remembering that Kirstie, when she came, would need it all. Then he took his pipe from his mouth, knocked out the ashes, wiped the stump on his sleeve, and put it in his pocket; took off his heavy boots, rolled himself in the coloured quilt, and tumbled comfortably into the bunk, untroubled by any thought of its previous tenants. No sooner was he still than the mice came out and began scampering across the loft. He felt the sound homely and companionable, and so fell asleep. As he slept the deep undreaming sleep of the wholesomely tired, the meagre fire burned low, sank into pulsating coals, and faded into blackness.

It was, perhaps, an hour later that Old Dave sat up, suddenly wide awake. He had no idea why he did it. He had heard no noise. He was certainly not afraid. There was no tremor in his seasoned nerves. Nevertheless, he was all at once absolutely awake, every sense alert. He felt almost as if there were some unkindred presence in the cabin. His first impulse was to spring from the bunk, and investigate. But, doubtless because he had spent so great a portion of his life in the forest, and because he had all that day been subtly played upon by its influences, another instinct triumphed. He followed the immemorial fashion of the folk of the wood, and just kept still, waiting to learn by watching.

He saw the two dim squares of the windows, and once imagined that one of them was for an instant shadowed. At this he smiled grimly there in the dark, well knowing that among all the forest-folk there was not one, not even the panther himself, so imprudent as to climb through a small window into a shut-up place, all reeking with the fresh and ominous scent of man.

Still he listened, in that movelessness which the haunted neighbourhood had taught him. The scurrying of the mice had ceased. There was no wind, and the darkness seemed all ears. The door, presently, gave a slow, gentle creaking, as if some heavy body pushed softly against it, trying the latch. The woodsman noiselessly reached out, and felt the handle of his axe, leaning by the head of the bunk. But the latch held, and the menacing furtive pressure was not repeated. Then, upon the very middle of the roof, began a scratching, a light rattling of claws, and footfalls went padding delicately over the bark. This puzzled the woodsman, who wondered how the owner of those clawed and velveted feet could have reached the roof without some noise of climbing. The soft tread, with an occasional scratch and snap, moved up and down the roof several times; and once, during a pause, a deep breath, ending with a sharp sniffing sound, was heard through the thin roof. Then came a muffled thud upon the chips, as of the drop of a heavy animal.

The spell was broken, and Old Dave rose from the bunk.

"It's jumped down off the roof! wild-cat, mebbe, or lynx. No painters 'round, 'tain't likely; though't did sound heavy fur a cat!" said he to himself, as he strode to the door, axe in hand.

Fearlessly he threw the door open, and looked out upon the glimmering night. The forest chill was in the air, the very breath and spirit of solitude. The mists gathered thickly a stone's throw from the cabin. He saw nothing that moved. He heard no stir. With a shrug of the shoulders he turned, latched the door again with just a trifle more exactness of precaution than before, lounged back to his bunk, and slept heedlessly till high dawn. A long finger of light, coldly rosy, came in through a broken pane to rouse him up.

When he went outside, the mists yet

clung white and chill about the clearing, and all the weed tops were beaded with thick dew. He noted that the chips were disturbed somewhat, but could find no definite track. Then, following a grassy path that led, through a young growth of alder, to the spring, he found signs. Down to the spring, and beyond, into the woods, a trail was drawn that spoke plain language to his wood-wise scrutiny. The grass was bent, the dew brushed off, by a body of some bulk and going close to the ground.

"Painter!" he muttered, knitting his brows, and casting a wary glance about him. "Reckon Kirstie'd better bring a gun along!"

All that day Dave Titus worked about the cabin and the barn. He mended the roof, patched the windows, rehung the door, filled the bunk — and the two similar ones in the smaller room — with aromatic fresh green spruce tips, and worked a miracle of rejuvenation upon the barn. He also cleaned out the spring, and chopped a handy pile of firewood. An old sheep-pen behind the barn he left in its ruins, saying to himself: —

"What with the b'ars, an' the painters, Kirstie ain't goin' to want to mess with sheep, I reckon. She'll have lots to do to look after her critters!"

By "critters" he meant the cow and the yoke of steers which were Kirstie Craig's property in the Settlement, and which, as he knew, she was to bring with her to her exile in the ancient wood.

That night, being now quite at home in the lonely cabin, and assured as to the stability of the door, Dave Titus slept dreamlessly from dark to dawn in the pleasant fragrance of his bunk. From dark to dawn the mice scurried in the loft, the bats flickered about the eaves, the unknown furry bulks leaned on the door or padded softly up and down the roof, but troubled not his rest. Then the wild folk began to take account of the fact that the sovereignty of the clearing had been resumed by man, and word of the new order went secretly about the forest. When, next morning, Dave Titus made careful survey of the clearing's skirts, calculating what brush and poles would be needed for Kirstie's fencing, making rough guesses at the acreage, and noting with approval the richness of the good brown soil, he thought himself alone. But he was not alone. Speculative eyes, large and small, fierce and timorous, from all the edges of the ancient wood kept watch on him.

Chapter III

The Exiles from the Settlement

LATE that afternoon Kirstie Craig arrived. Her coming was a migration.

The first announcement of her approach was the dull *tank*, *tank*, *a-tonk*, *tank* of cow-bells down the trail, at sound of which Old Dave threw aside his axe and slouched away to meet her. There was heard a boy's voice shouting with young authority, "Gee! Gee, Bright! Gee, Star!" and the head of the procession came into view in the solemn green archway of the woods.

The head of the procession was Kirstie Craig herself, a tall, erect, strong-stepping, long-limbed woman in blue-grey homespuns, with a vivid scarlet kerchief tied over her head. She was leading, by a rope about its horns, a meekly tolerant black-and-white cow. To her left hand clung a skipping little figure in a pink calico frock, a broad-brimmed hat of coarse straw flung back from her hair and hanging by ribbons from her neck. This was the five-year-old Miranda, Kirstie Craig's daughter. She had ridden most of the journey, and now was full of excited interest over the approach to her new home. Following close behind came the yoke of long-horned, mild-eyed steers, — Bright, a light sorrel, and Star, a curious red-and-black brindle with a radiating splash of white in the middle of his forehead. These, lurching heavily on the yoke, were hauling a rude "drag," on which was lashed the meagre pile of Kirstie's belongings and supplies. Close at Star's heaving flank walked a lank and tow-haired boy from the Settlement, his long ox-goad in hand, and an expression of resigned dissatisfaction on his grey-eyed, ruddy young face. Liking, and thoroughly believing in, Kirstie Craig, he had impulsively yielded to her request, and let himself be hired to assist her flight into exile. But in so doing he had gone roughly counter to public opinion; for the Settlement, though stupidly inhospitable to Kirstie Craig, none the less resented her decision to leave it. Her scheme of occupying the deserted cabin, farming the deserted clearing, and living altogether aloof from her unloved and unloving fellows, was scouted on every hand as the freak of a madwoman; and Young Dave, just coming to the age when public opinion begins to seem important, felt uneasy at being identified with a matter of public ridicule. He saw himself already, in imagination, a theme for the fine wit of the Settlement. Nevertheless, he was glad to be helping Kirstie, for he was sound and fearless at heart, and he counted her a true friend if she did seem to him a bit queer. He was faithful, but disapproving. It was Old Dave alone, his father, who backed the woman's venture without criticism or demur. He had known Kirstie from small girlhood, and known her for a brave, loyal, silent, strongly-enduring soul; and in his eyes she did well to leave the Settlement, where a shallow spite, sharpened by her proud reticence and supplied with arrows of injury by her misfortunes, made life an undesisting and immitigable hurt to her.

As she emerged from the twilight and came out upon the sunny bleakness of the clearing, the unspeakable loneliness of it struck a sudden pallor into her grave dark face. For a moment, even the humanity that was hostile to her seemed less cruel than this voiceless solitude. Then her resolution came back. The noble but somewhat immobile lines of her large features relaxed into a half smile at her own weakness. She took possession, as it were, by a sweeping gesture of her head; then silently gave her hand in greeting to Old Dave, who had ranged up beside her and swung the dancing Miranda to his shoulder. Nothing was said for several moments, as the party moved slowly up the slope; for they were folk of few words, these people, not praters like so many of their fellows in the Settlement.

At last the pink frock began to wriggle on the lumberman's shoulder, and Miranda cried out:—

"Let me down, Uncle Dave, I want to pick those pretty flowers for my mother."

The crimson glories of the fireweed had filled her eyes with delight; and in a few minutes she was struggling after the procession with her small arms full of the long-stalked blooms.

In front of the cabin door the procession stopped. Dave turned, and said seriously: —

"I've done the best I could by ye, Kirstie; an' I reckon it ain't so bad a site for ye, after all. But ye'll be powerful lonesome."

"Thank you kindly, Dave. But we ain't going to be lonesome, Miranda and me."

"But there's painters 'round. You'd ought to hev a gun, Kirstie. I'll be sackin' out some stuff fur ye nex' week, Davey an' me, an' I reckon as how I'd better fetch ye a gun."

"We'll be right hungry for a sight of your faces by that time, Dave," said Kirstie, sweeping a look of tenderness over the boy's face, where he stood leaning on Star's brindled shoulder. "But I ain't scared of panthers. Don't you mind about the gun, now, for I don't want it, and I won't use it!"

"She ain't skeered o' nothin' that walks," muttered Young Dave, with admiration.

The strong face darkened.

"Yes, I am, Davey," she answered; "I'm afeard of evil tongues."

"Well, my girl, here ye're well quit of 'em," said the old lumberman, a slow anger burning on his rough-hewn face as he thought of certain busy backbiters in the Settlement.

Just then Miranda's small voice chimed in.

"Oh, Davey," she cried, catching gleefully at the boy's leg, "look at the nice, great big dog!" And her little brown finger pointed to a cluster of stumps, of all shapes and sizes, far over on the limits of the clearing. Her wide, brown eyes danced elvishly. The others followed her gaze, all staring intently; but they saw no excuse for her excitement.

"It might be a b'ar she sees," said Old Dave; "but I can't spot it."

"They're plenty hereabouts, I suppose," said Kirstie, rather indifferently, letting her eyes wander to other portions of her domain.

"Ain't no bear there," asserted Young Dave, with all the confidence of his years. "It's a stump!"

"Nice big dog! I want it, mother," piped Miranda, suddenly darting away. But her mother's firm hand fell upon her shoulder.

"There's no big dog out here, child," she said quietly. And Old Dave, after puckering his keen eyes and knitting his shaggy brows in vain, exclaimed: —

"Oh, quit yer foolin', Mirandy, ye little witch. 'Tain't nothin' but stumps, I tell ye."

It was the child's eyes, however, that had the keener vision, the subtler knowledge; and, though now she let herself seem to be persuaded, and obediently carried her armful of fireweed into the cabin, she knew it was no stump she had been looking at. And as for Kroof, the she-bear, though she had indeed sat moveless as a stump among the stumps, she knew that the child had detected her. She saw that Miranda had the eyes that see everything and cannot be deceived.

For two days the man and the boy stayed at the clearing to help Kirstie get settled. The fields rang pleasantly with the *tank*, *tank*, *a-tonk*, *tank* of the cow-bells, as the cattle fed over the new pasturage. The edges of the clearing resounded with axe strokes, and busy voices echoed on the autumn air. There was much rough fencing to be built, — zig-zag arrangements of brush and saplings, — in order that Kirstie's "critters" might be shut in till the sense of home should so grow upon them as to keep them from straying.

The two days done, Old Dave and Young Dave shouldered their axes and went away. Kirstie forthwith straightened her fine shoulders to the Atlas load of solitude which had threatened at first to overwhelm her; and she and Miranda settled down to a strangely silent routine. This was broken, however, at first, by weekly visits from Old Dave, who came to bring hay, and roots, and other provisions against the winter, together with large "hanks" of coarse homespun yarn, to occupy Kirstie's fingers during the long winter evenings.

Kirstie was well fitted to the task she had so bravely set herself. She could swing an axe; and the fencing grew steadily through the fall. She could guide the plough; and before the snow came some ten acres of the long fallow sod had been turned up in brown furrows, to be ripened and mellowed by the frosts for next spring's planting. The black-and-white cow was still in good milk, and could be depended on not to go dry a day more than two months before calving. The steers were thrifty and sleek, and showed no signs of fretting for old pastures. The hoarse but homely music of the cow-bells, sounding all day over the fields, and giving out an occasional soft *tonk-a-tonk* from the darkness of the stalls at night, came to content her greatly. The lines which she had brought from the Settlement smoothed themselves from about her mouth and eyes, and the large, sufficing beauty of her face was revealed in the peace of her new life.

About seven years before this move to the cabin in the clearing, Kirstie Craig— then Kirstie MacAlister — had gone one evening to the cross-roads grocery which served the Settlement as General Intelligence Office. Here was the post-office as well, in a corner of the store, fitted up with some dozen of lettered and dusty pigeon-holes. Nodding soberly to the loafers who lounged about on the soap boxes and nail kegs, Kirstie stepped up to the counter to buy a quart of molasses. She was just passing over her gaudy blue-and-yellow pitcher to be filled, when a stranger came in who caught her attention. He did far more than catch her attention; for the stately and sombre girl, who had never before taken pains to look twice on any man's face, now felt herself grow hot and cold as this stranger's eyes glanced carelessly over her splendid form. She heard him ask the postmaster for lodgings. He spoke in a tired voice, and accents that set him apart from the men of the Settlement. She looked at him twice and yet again, noted with a pang that he seemed ill, and met his eye fairly for just one heart-beat. At once she flushed scarlet under it, snatched up her pitcher, and almost rushed from the store. The loafers were too much occupied with the new arrival to notice her perturbation; but he noticed it, and was pleased. Never before had he seen so splendid a girl as this black-haired, sphinx-faced creature, with the scarlet kerchief about her head. She was a picture that awoke the artist in him, and put him in haste to resume his palette and brushes.

For Frank Craig, dilettante and man of the world, was a good deal of an artist when the mood seized him strongly enough. When another mood seized him, with sufficient vigour to overcome his native indolence, he was something of a musician; and again, more rarely, something of a poet. The temperament was his; but the steadiness of purpose, the decision of will, the long-enduring patience, these were not. He had just enough money to let him float through his world without work. Health he had not, and the poor semblance of it which mere youth supplied he had squandered childishly. Hearing of new health in the gift of the northern spruce woods, with their high, balsam-sweet airs, he had drifted away from his temptations, and at last sought out this remote backwoods settlement as a place where he might expect to get much for little. He was very good to look upon,—about as tall as Kirstie herself,—slender, active, alert in movement when not wearied, thoroughbred in every line of face and figure. His eyes, of a very deep greyish green under long black lashes, were penetrating in their clearness, but curiously unstable. In their beautiful depths there was waged forever a strange conflict between honesty and inconstancy. His face, pale and sallow, was clothed with a trimly pointed, close, dark beard; and his hair, just a trifle more abundant than the fashion of his world approved, was of a peculiar, tawny dark bronze.

The air of the Settlement was healing and tonic to the lungs, and before he had breathed it a month he felt himself aglow with joyous life. Before he had breathed it a month he had won Kirstie MacAlister, to whom he seemed little less than a god. To him, on her part, she was a splendid mystery. Even her peculiarities of grammar and accent did no more than lend a piquancy to her strangeness. They appealed as a rough, fresh flavour to his wearied senses. Here, safe from the wasting world, he would really paint, would really write, and life would come to mean something. One day he and Kirstie went away on the rattling old mail-waggon, which visited the Settlement twice a week. Ten days later they came back as man and wife, whereat the Settlement showed no surprise whatever.

For a whole year after the birth of his child, the great-eyed and fairy-like Miranda, Frank Craig stayed at the Settlement, seemingly content. He was loving, admiring, tactful, proud of his dark impressive wife, and the quickness with which she caught his purity of speech. Then one day he seemed restless. He talked of business in the city — of a month's absence that could not be avoided. With a kind of terror at her heart Kirstie heard him, but offered no hint of opposition to so reasonable a purpose. And by the next trip of the rattling mail-waggon he went, leaving the Settlement dark to Kirstie's eyes.

But — he never came back. The months rolled by and no word came of him; and Kirstie gnawed her heart out in proud anguish. Inquiry throughout the cities of the coast brought no hint of him. Then, as the months climbed into years, that tender humanity which resents misfortune as a crime started a rumour that Kirstie had been fooled. Perhaps there had been no marriage, went the whisper at first. "Served her right, with her airs, thinkin' she could ketch a gentleman!" — was the next development of it. Kirstie, with her superior air, had never been popular at best; and after her marriage the sufficiency and exclusiveness of her joy, coupled with the comparative fineness of speech which she adopted, made her the object of jealous criticism through all the country-side. When the temple of her soaring happiness came down about her ears, then was the time for her chastening, and the gossips of the Settlement took a hand in it with right good-will. Nothing else worth talking about happened in that neighbourhood during the next few years, so the little rumour was cherished and nourished. Presently it grew to a great scandal, and the gossips came to persuade themselves that things had not been as they should be. Kirstie, they said, was being very properly punished by Providence, and it was well to show that they, chaste souls, stood on the side of Providence. If Providence threw a stone, it was surely their place to throw three.

At last some one of imagination vivid beyond that of the common run added a new feature. Some one else had heard from some one else of some one having seen Frank Craig in the city. There was at first a difference of opinion as to what city; but that little discrepancy was soon smoothed out. Then a woman was suggested, and forthwith it appeared that he had been seen driving with a handsome woman, behind a spanking pair, with liveried coachman and footman on the box. Thus gradually the myth acquired a colour to endear it to the unoccupied rural imagination. Kirstie's inquiries soon proved to her the utter baselessness of the scandal; but she was too proud to refute what she knew to be a cherished lie. She endured, for Miranda's sake, till the dark face grew lined, and the black eyes smouldered dangerously, and she began to fear lest she should do some one a hurt. At last, having heard by chance of that deserted clearing in the forest, she sold out her cottage at a sacrifice and fled from the bitter tongues.

Chapter IV

Miranda and the Furtive Folk

FROM the very first day of her new life at the clearing, Miranda had found it to her taste. Her mother loved it for its peace, for its healing; but to the elvish child it had an incomparably deeper and more positive appeal. For her the place was not solitary. Her wide eyes saw what Kirstie could not see; and to her the forest edges — which she was not allowed to pass — were full of most satisfying playmates just waiting for her to invite their confidence. Meanwhile, she had the two steers and the black-and-white cow to talk to. Her mother noticed that when she sat down in the grass by the head of one of the animals, and began her low mysterious communication, it would stop its feeding and hearken motionless. The black-and-red brindle, Star, would sometimes follow her about like a dog, as if spelled by the child's solemn eyes. Then the solemn eyes on a sudden would dance with light; her lips would break into a peal of whimsical mirth, shrill but not loud; and the steer, with a flick of his tail and an offended snort, would turn again to his pasturing.

In a hole in one of the logs, just under the eaves of the cabin, there was a family of red squirrels, the four youngsters about three-fourths grown and almost ready to shift for themselves. No sooner had the old lumberman and his son gone away than the squirrels began to make themselves much at home. They saw in Kirstie a huge and harmless creature, whose presence in the cabin was useful to scare away their enemies. But in Miranda they found a sort of puzzling kinship. The two old squirrels would twitch up and down on the edge of the roof, chattering shrilly to her, flirting their airy tails, and stretching down their heads to scan her searchingly with their keen protruding eyes; while Miranda, just below, would dance excitedly up and down in response, nodding her head, jerking her elbows, and chattering back at them in a quick, shrill voice. It was a very different voice to the soft murmurs in which she talked to the cattle; but to the squirrels it appeared satisfactory. Before she had been a week at the clearing the whole squirrel family seemed to regard her as one of themselves, snatching bread from her tiny brown fingers, and running up her skirt to her shoulder whensoever the freak possessed them. Kirstie, they ignored—the harmless, necessary Kirstie, mother to Miranda.

No sooner were they fairly settled than the child discovered an incongruity in her gay pink calico frocks, and got her mother to bury them out of sight in the deal chest behind the door. She was at ease now only in the dull, blue-grey homespun, which made her feel at one with her quiet surroundings. Nevertheless the vein of contradiction which streaked her baby heart with bright inconsistencies bade her demand always a bit of scarlet ribbon about her neck. This whim Kirstie humoured with a smile, recognizing in it a perpetuation of the scarlet kerchief about her own black hair. As for Miranda's hair, it was black like her mother's when seen in shadow; but in the sunshine it showed certain tawny lights, a pledge of her fatherhood to all who had known Frank Craig.

So the autumn slipped by; and the silent folk of the wood, watching her curiously and unwinkingly as she played while her mother built fences, came to know Miranda as a creature in some way not quite alien to themselves. They knew that she often saw them when her mother's eyes could not. Perceiving that her mother did not quite understand her, at times, when she tried to point out pretty animals among the trees, the child grew a little sensitive and reticent on the subject; and the furtive folk, who had at first inclined to resent her inescapable vision, presently realized her reserves and were appeased. Her grey little sprite of a figure might have darted in among the trees, turned to a statue, and become suddenly as invisible as any lynx, or cat, or hare, or pine-marten amongst them, except, indeed, for that disquieting flame of scarlet at her neck. This was a puzzle to all the folk of the wood, continually reminding them that this quiet-flitting creature did not really belong to the wood at all, but to the great woman with the red about her head, whose axe made so vexing a clamour amid the trees. As for Kroof, the bear, that bit of scarlet so interested her that one day, being curious, she came much nearer than she intended. Miranda saw her, of course, and gazed with wide-eyed longing for the "great big dog" as a playmate. Just then Kirstie saw her, too — very close at hand, and very huge.

For the first time, Kirstie Craig felt something like fear, not for herself, but for the child. Thrusting Miranda roughly behind her, she clutched her axe, and stood motionless, erect and formidable, awaiting attack. Her great black eyes blazed ominously upon the intruder. But

Kroof, well filled with late berries, and sweet wild roots, and honeycomb, was in most amiable humour, and just shambled off lazily when she saw herself detected; whereupon Kirstie, with a short laugh of relief, threw down her axe and snatched the child to her breast. Miranda, however, was weeping salt tears of disappointment.

"I want it, mother," she sobbed; "the nice big dog. You scared it away."

Kirstie had heard more than enough about the dog.

"Hark now, Miranda," she said severely, giving her shoulder a slight shake to enforce attention. "You just remember what I say. That ain't a dog; that's a bear; *a bear*, I say! And don't you ever go near it, or it'll eat you up. Mind you now, Miranda, or I'll just whip you well."

Kirstie was a little fluttered and thrown off her poise at the idea of Miranda encountering the great animal alone, and perhaps attempting to bring it home to play with; so she forgot for a moment the wonted stringency of her logic. As for Miranda, she consented to obey, and held her tongue; but she clung secretly to her own opinion on the subject of the big dog. She knew very well that the fascinating animal did not want to eat her; and her mother's order seemed to her just one of those bits of maternal perversity which nobody can ever hope to understand.

The incident, however, overshadowed the child's buoyant spirits for the best part of two whole days. It thrust so very far off the time she hoped for, when she might know and talk to the shy, furtive folk of the wood, with their strange, unwinking eyes. Her mother kept her now ever close to her skirts. She had no one to talk to about the things her mother did not understand, except the steers and the black-and-white cow, and the rather irrepressible squirrels.

The winter, which presently fell white and soundless and sparkling about the lonely cabin, was to Miranda full of events. Before the snow Kirstie had repaired the old lean-to, turning it into a fowl-house; and now they had six prim hens to occupy it, and a splendid, flame-red cock who crowed most loftily. Miranda felt that this proud bird despised her, so she did not get on very well with him; but the hens were amiable, if uninteresting, and it was a perennial joy to search out their eggs in the loft or the corners of the stalls. Then there were the paths to be kept clear after every snow-fall, — the path to the spring, the path to the barn door and hen-house, the path to the woodpile. Uncle Dave had made her a hand-sled, and she had the exhilarating duty of hauling in the wood from the pile as fast as her mother could split it. It was a spirited race, this, in which her mother somehow always managed to keep just about one stick ahead.

And the fishing — this was a great event, coming about once a week, if the weather suited. Both Kirstie and Miranda were semi-vegetarians. Frank Craig had been a decryer of flesh-meat, one who would have chosen to live on fruits and roots and grains and eggs, had not his body cried out against the theory of his brain. But he had so far infected his wife with his prejudice that neither she nor the child now touched meat in any form. The aversion, artificial on Kirstie's part, was instinctive on Miranda's. But as for fish —fish seemed to them both quite another matter. Even Miranda of the sympathies and the perceptions had no sense of fellowship for these cold-blooded, clammy, unpleasant things. She had a fierce little delight in catching them; she had a contented joy in eating them when fried to a savory brown in butter and yellow cornmeal. For Miranda was very close to Nature, and Nature laughs at consistency.

The fishing in which Miranda so delighted took place in winter at the lake. When the weather seemed quite settled, Kirstie would set out on her strong snowshoes, with Miranda, on her fairy facsimiles of them, striding bravely beside her, and follow the long, white trail down to the lake. Even to Miranda's discerning eyes the trail was lonely now, for most of the forest folk were either asleep, or abroad, or fearful lest their tinted coats should reveal them against the snowy surface. Once in a while she detected the hare squatting under a spruce bush, looking like a figure of snow in his winter coat; and once or twice, too, she saw the weasel, white now, with but a black tip to his tail as a warning to all who had cause to dread his cruelty. Miranda knew nothing about him, but she did not quite like the weasel, which was just as well, seeing that the weasel hated Miranda and all the world besides. As for the lynx and the brown cat, they kept warily aloof in their winter shyness. The wood-mice were asleep, — warm, furry balls buried in their dry nests far from sight; and Kroof, too, was dreaming away the frozen months in a hollow under a pine root, with five or six feet of snow drifted over her door to keep her sleep unjarred.

Arrived at the lake, Kirstie would cut two holes through the ice with her nimble axe, bait two hooks with bits of fat pork, and put a line into Miranda's little mittened hands. The trout in the lake were numerous and hungry; and somehow Miranda's hook had ever the more deadly fascination for them, and Miranda's catch would outnumber Kirstie's by often three to one. Though her whole small being seemed absorbed in the fierce game, Miranda was all the time vividly aware of the white immensity enfolding her. The lifeless white level of the lake; the encircling shores all white; the higher fringe of trees, black beneath, but deeply garmented with white; the steep mountain-side, at the foot of the lake, all white; and over-brooding, glimmering, opalescent, fathomless, the flat white arch of sky. Across the whiteness of the mountain-side, one day, Miranda saw a dark beast moving, a beast that looked to her like a great cat. She saw it halt, gazing down at them; and even at that distance she could see it stretch wide its formidable jaws. A second more and she heard the cry which came from those formidable jaws, — a high, harsh, screeching wail, which amused her so that she forgot to land a fish. But her mother seemed troubled at the sound. She gazed very steadily for some seconds at the far-off shape, and then said: "Panthers, Miranda! I don't mind bears; but with panthers we've got to keep our eyes open. I reckon we'll get home before sundown to-day; and mind you keep right close by me every step."

All this solicitude seemed to Miranda a lamentable mistake. She had no doubt in her own mind that the panther would be nice to play with.

As I have said, the winter was for Miranda full of events. Twice, as she was carrying out the morning dish of hot potatoes and meal to the hens, she saw Ten-Tine, the bull caribou, cross the clearing with measured stately tread, his curious, patchy antlers held high, his muzzle stretched straight ahead of him, his demure cows at his heels. This was before the snow lay deep in the forest. Later on in the winter she would look out with eager interest every morning to see what visitors had been about the cabin during the night. Sometimes there was a fox track, very dainty, cleanly indented, and regular, showing that the animal who made it knew where he was going and had something definite in view. Hare tracks there were sure to be — she soon came to recognize those three-toed, triplicate clusters of impressions, stamped deeply upon the snow by the long, elastic jump. Whenever there was a weasel track, — narrow, finely pointed, treacherously innocent, — it was sure to be closely parallel to that of a leaping hare; and Miranda soon apprehended, by that instinct of hers, that the companionship was not like to be well for the hare. Once, to her horror, she found that a hare track ended suddenly, right under the cabin window, in a blood-stained patch, bestrewn with fur and bones. All about it the snow was swept as if by wings, and two strange footprints told the story. They were long, these two footprints — forked, with deep hooks for toes, and an obscure sort of brush mark behind them. This was where the owl had sat up on the snow for a few minutes after dining, to ponder on the merits of the general order of things, and of a good meal in particular. Miranda's imagination painted a picture of the big bird sitting there in the moonlight beside the bloody bones, his round, horned head turning slowly from one side to the other, his hooked beak snapping now and again in reminiscence, his sharp eyes wide open and flaming. There was also the track of a fox, which had come up from the direction of the barn, investigated the scene of action, and gone off at a sharp, decisive angle toward the woods. Miranda had no clew to tell her how stealthily that fox had come, or how nearly he had succeeded in catching an owl for his breakfast; but from that morning she bore a grudge against owls, and never could hear without a flash of wrath their hollow *two-hoo-hoo-whoo-oo* echoing solemnly from the heart of the pinewood.

But the owl was not the only bird that Miranda knew that winter. Well along in January, when the haws were all gone, and most of the withered rowan-berries had been eaten, and famine threatened such of the bird-folk as had not journeyed south, there came to the cabin brisk foraging flocks of the ivory-billed snow-bird. For these Miranda had crumbs ready always, and as word of her bounty went abroad in the forest, her feathered pensioners increased. Even a hungry crow would come now and then, glossy and sideling, watchful and audacious, to share the hospitality of this kind Miranda of the crumbs. She liked the crows, and would hear no ill of them from her mother; but most of all she liked those big, rosy-headed, trustful children, the pine-grosbeaks, who would almost let her take them in her hands. Whenever their wandering flocks came down to her, she held winter carnival for them.

During those days when it was not fine enough to go out, — when the snow drove in great swirls and phantom armies across the open, and a dull roar came from the straining forest, and the fowls went to roost at midday, and the cattle munched contentedly in their stanchions, glad to be shut in,—then the cabin seemed very pleasant to Miranda. On such days the drifts were sometimes piled halfway up the windows. On such days the dry logs on the hearth blazed more brightly than their wont, and the flames sang more merrily up the chimney. On such days the piles of hot buckwheat cakes, drenched in butter and brown molasses, tasted more richly toothsome than at any time else, and on such days she learned to knit. This was very interesting. At first she knit gay black-and-red garters for her mother; and then, speedily mastering this rudimentary process, she was fairly launched on a stocking, with four needles. The stocking, of course, was for her mother, who would not find fault if it were knitted too tightly here and too loosely there. As for Kirstie herself, her nimble needles would click all day, turning out socks and mittens of wonderful thickness to supply the steady market of the lumber camps.

One night, after just such a cosey, shut-in day, Miranda was awakened by a scratching sound on the roof. Throughout the cold weather Miranda slept with her mother in the main room, in a broad new bunk which had been substituted for the narrow one wherein Old Dave had slept on his first visit to the clearing. Miranda caught her mother's arm, and shook it gently. But Kirstie was already awake, lying with wide eyes, listening.

"What's that, mother, trying to get in?" asked the child in a whisper.

"Hush-sh-sh," replied Kirstie, laying her fingers on the child's mouth.

The scratching came louder now, as the light snow was swept clear and the inquisitive claws reached the bark. Then it stopped. After a second or two of silence there was a loud, blowing sound, as if the visitor were clearing his nostrils from the snow and cold. This was followed by two or three long, penetrating sniffs, so curiously hungry in their suggestion that even Miranda's dauntless little heart beat very fast. As for Kirstie, she was decidedly nervous. Springing out of bed she ran to the hearth, raked the coals from the ashes, fanned them, heaped on birch bark and dry wood, and in a moment had a great blaze roaring up the chimney-throat. The glow from the windows streamed far out across the snow. To the visitor it proved disconcerting. There was one more sharp rattle of claws upon the roof, then a fluffy thump below the eaves. The snow had stopped falling hours before; and when, at daylight, Kirstie opened the door, there was the deep hollow where the panther had jumped down, and there was the floundering trail where he had fled.

This incident made Miranda amend, in some degree, her first opinion of panthers.

Chapter V

Kroof, the She-bear

SPRING came early to the clearing that year. Kirstie's autumn furrows, dark and steaming, began to show in patches through the diminished snow. The chips before the house and the litter about the barn, drawing the sun strongly, were first of all uncovered; and over them, as to the conquest of new worlds, the haughty cock led forth his dames to scratch. "Saunders," Miranda had called him, in remembrance of a strutting beau at the Settlement; and with the advent of April cheer, and an increasing abundance of eggs, and an ever resounding cackle from his complacent partlets, his conceit became insufferable. One morning, when something she did offended his dignity, he had the presumption to face her with beak advanced and wide-ruffled neck feathers. But Saunders did not know Miranda. Quick as a flash of light she seized him by the legs, whirled him around her head, and flung him headlong, squawking with fear and shame, upon his own dunghill. It took him a good hour to recover his self-esteem, but after that Miranda stood out in his eyes as the one creature in the world to be respected.

When the clearing was quite bare, except along the edges of the forest, and Kirstie was again at work on her fencing, the black-and-white cow gave birth to a black-and-white calf, which Miranda at once claimed as her own property. It was a very wobbly, knock-kneed little heifer; but Miranda admired it immensely, and with lofty disregard of its sex, christened it Michael.

About this time the snow shrank away from her hollow under the pine root, and Kroof came forth to sun herself. She had lived all winter on nothing but the fat stored up on the spaces of her capacious frame. Nevertheless she was not famished — she had still a reserve to come and go on, till food should be abundant. A few days after waking up she bore a cub. It was the custom of her kind to bear two cubs at a birth; but Kroof, besides being by long odds the biggest she-bear ever known in that region, had a pronounced individuality of her own, and was just as well satisfied with herself over one cub as over two.

The hollow under the pine root was warm and softly lined — a condition quite indispensable to the newcomer, which was about as unlike a bear as any baby creature of its size could well manage to be. It was blind, helpless, whimpering, more shapeless and clumsy-looking than the clumsiest conceivable pup, and almost naked. Its tender, hairless hide looked a poor thing to confront the world with; but its appetite was astounding, and Kroof's milk inexhaustible. In a few days a soft dark fur began to appear. As the mother sat, hour by hour, watching it and suckling it, half erect upon her haunches, her fore legs braced wide apart, her head stretched as far down as possible, her narrow red tongue hanging out to one side, her eyes half closed in rapture, it seemed to grow visibly beneath her absorbing gaze. Before four weeks had passed, the cub was covered with a jet black coat, soft and glossy. This being the case, he thought it time to open his eyes and look about.

He was now about the size of a small cat, but of a much heavier build. His head, at this age, was shorter for its breadth than his mother's; the ears much larger, fan-like and conspicuous. His eyes, very softly vague at first, soon acquired a humorous, mischievous expression, which went aptly with the erect, inquisitive ears. Altogether he was a fine baby — a fair justification of Kroof's pride.

The spring being now fairly forward, and pale, whitish-green shoots upthrusting themselves numerously through the dead leaves, and the big crimson leaf-bud of the skunk-cabbage vividly punctuating the sombreness of the swamp, Kroof led her infant forth to view their world. He had no such severe and continued education to undergo as that which falls to the lot of other youngsters among the folk of the ancient wood. For those others the first lesson, the hardest and the most tremendous in its necessity, was how to avoid their enemies. With this lesson ill-learned, all others found brief term; for the noiseless drama, in which all the folk of the forest had their parts, moved ever, through few scenes or through many, to a tragic close. But the bear, being for the most part dominant, had his immunities. Even the panther, swift and fierce and masterful, never deliberately sought quarrel with the bear, being mindful of his disastrous clutch and the lightning sweep of his paw. The bear-cub, therefore, going with its mother till almost full grown, gave no thought at all to enemies; and the cub with such a giantess as Kroof for its mother might safely make a mock even at panthers. Kroof's cub had thus but simple things to learn, following close at his mother's flank. During the first blind weeks of his cubhood he had, indeed, to acquire the prime virtue of silence, which was not easy, for he loved to whimper and grumble in a comfortable little fashion of his own. This was all right while Kroof was at home; but when she was out foraging, then silence was the thing. This he learned, partly from Kroof's admonitions, partly from a deep-seated instinct; and whenever he was left alone, he held his tongue. There was always the possibility, slight but unpleasant, of a fox or a brown cat noting Kroof's absence, and seizing the chance to savour a delicate morsel of sucking bear.

Wandering the silent woods with Kroof, the cub would sniff carefully at the moist earth and budding shoots wheresoever his mother stopped to dig. He thus learned where to find the starchy roots which form so large a part of the bear's food in spring. He found out the important difference between the sweet groundnuts and the fiery bitter bulb of the arum, or Indian turnip; and he learned to go over the grassy meadows by the lake and dig unerringly for the wild bean's nourishing tubers. He discovered, also, what old stumps to tear apart when he wanted a pleasantly acid tonic dose of the larvæ of the wood-ant. Among these serious occupations he would gambol between his mother's feet, or caper hilariously on his hind legs. Soon he would have been taught to detect a bee tree, and to rob it of its delectable stores without getting his eyes stung out; but just then the mysterious forest fates dropped the curtain on his merry little play, as a reminder that not even for the great black bear could the rule of doom be relaxed.

Kroof's first wanderings with the cub were in the neighbourhood of the clearing, where both were sometimes seen by Miranda. The sight of the cub so overjoyed her that she departed from her usual reticence as to the forest-folk, and told her mother about the lovely, glossy little dog that the nice, great big dog took about with her. The only result was that Kirstie gave her a sharp warning.

"Dog!" she exclaimed severely; "didn't I tell you, Miranda, it was a bear? Bears are mostly harmless, if you leave them alone; but an old bear with a cub is mighty ugly. Mind what I say now, you keep by me and don't go too nigh the edge of the woods."

And so, for the next few weeks, Miranda was watched very strictly, lest her childish daring should involve her with the bears.

Along in the summer Kroof began to lead the cub wider afield. The longer journeys vexed the little animal at first, and tired him; so that sometimes he would throw himself down on his back, with pinky-white soles of protest in the air, and refuse to go a step farther. But in spite of the appeal of his quizzical little black snout, big ears, and twinkling eyes, old Kroof would box him sternly till he was glad enough to jump up and renew the march. With the exercise he got a little leaner, but much harder, and soon came to delight in the widest wandering. Nothing could tire him, and at the end of the journey he would chase rabbits, or weasels, or other elusive creatures, till convicted of futility by his mother's sarcastic comments.

These wide wanderings were, indeed, the making of him, so that he promised to rival Kroof herself in prowess and stature; but alas! poor cub, they were also his undoing. Had he stayed at home — but even that might have little availed, for among the folk of the wood it is right at home that fate most surely strikes.

One day they two were exploring far over in the next valley — the valley of the Quah-Davic, a tract little familiar to Kroof herself. At the noon hour Kroof lay down in a little hollow of coolness beside a spring that *drip-drop, drip-drop, drip-dropped* from the face of a green rock. The cub, however, went untiringly exploring the thickets for fifty yards about, out of sight, indeed, but scrupulously never out of ear-shot.

Near one of these thickets his nostrils caught a new and enthralling savour. He had never, in his brief life, smelled anything at all like it, but an unerring instinct told him it was the smell of something very good to eat. Pushing through the leafage he came upon the source of the fragrance. Under a slanting structure of logs he found a piece of flesh, yellowish-white, streaked thickly with dark reddish-brown,—and, oh, so sweet smelling! It was stuck temptingly on a forked point of wood. His ears stood up very wide and high in his eagerness. His sensitive nostrils wrinkled as he sniffed at the tempting find. He decided that he would just taste it, and then go fetch his mother. But it was a little high up for him. He rose, set his small white teeth into it, clutched it with his soft forepaws, and flung his whole weight upon it to pull it down.

Kroof, dozing in her hollow of coolness, heard a small agonized screech, cut short horribly. On the instant her great body went tearing in a panic through the underbrush. She found poor cub crushed flat under the huge timbers of "a dead-fall," his glossy head and one paw sticking out piteously, his little red tongue protruding from his distorted mouth.

Kroof needed no second look to know

in her heart he was dead, stone dead; but in the rage of her grief she would not acknowledge it. She tore madly at the great timber,—so huge a thing to set to crush so small a life,—and so astonishing was the strength of her claws and her vast forearms that in the course of half an hour she had the trap fairly demolished. Softly she removed the crushed and shapeless body, licking the mouth, the nostrils, the pitifully staring eyes; snuggling it lightly as a breath, and moaning over it. She would lift the head a little with her paw, and redouble her caresses as it fell limply aside. Then it grew cold. This was testimony she could not pretend to ignore. She ceased the caresses which proved so vain to keep warmth in the little body she loved. With her snout held high in air she turned around slowly twice, as if in an appeal to some power not clearly apprehended; then, without another glance at her dead, she rushed off madly through the forest.

All night she wandered aimlessly, hither and thither through the low Quah-Davic valley, over the lower slopes of the mountain, through tracts where she had never been, but of which she took no note; and toward noon of the following day she found herself once more in the ancient wood, not far from the clearing. She avoided widely the old den under the pine root, and at last threw herself down, worn out and with unsuckled teats fiercely aching, behind the trunk of a fallen hemlock.

She slept heavily for an hour or two. Then she was awakened by the crying of a child. She knew it at once for Miranda's voice; and being in some way stirred by it, in spite of the preoccupation of her pain, she got up and moved noiselessly toward the sound.

Chapter VI

The Initiation of Miranda

THAT same day, just after noon-meat, when Miranda had gone out with the scraps in a yellow bowl to feed the hens, Kirstie had been taken with what the people at the Settlement would have called "a turn." All the morning she had felt unusually oppressed by the heat, but had thought little of it. Now, as she was wiping the dishes, she quite unaccountably dropped one of them on the floor. The crash aroused her. She saw with a pang that it was Miranda's little plate of many colours. Then things turned black about her. She just managed to reel across to the bunk, and straightway fell upon it in a kind of faint. From this state she passed into a heavy sleep, which lasted for several hours, and probably saved her from some violent sickness.

When Miranda had fed the hens she did not go straight back to her mother. Instead, she wandered off toward the edge of the dark firwood, where it came down close behind the cabin. The broad light of the open fields, now green with buckwheat, threw a living illumination far in among the cool arcades.

Between the straight grey trunks Miranda's clear eyes saw something move. She liked it very much indeed. It looked to her extremely like a cat, only larger than any cat she had seen at the Settlement, taller on its legs, and with a queer, thick stump of a tail. In fact, it was a cat, the brown cat, or lesser lynx. Its coat was a red brown, finely mottled with a paler shade. It had straight brushes of bristles on the tips of its ears, like its big cousin, the Canada lynx, only much less conspicuous than his; and the expression on the moonlike round of its face was both fierce and shy. But it was a cat, plainly enough; and Miranda's heart went out to it, as it sat up there in the shadows, watching her steadily with wide pale eyes.

"Oh, pretty pussy! pretty pussy!" called Miranda, stretching out her hands to it coaxingly, and running into the wood.

The brown cat waited unwinking till she was about ten paces off, then turned and darted deeper into the shadows. When it was all but out of sight it stopped, turned again, and sat up to watch the eager child. It seemed curious as to the bit of scarlet at her neck. Miranda was now absorbed in the pursuit, and sanguine of catching the beautiful pussy. This time she was suffered to come almost within grasping distance, before the animal again wheeled with an angry *pfuff* and darted away. Disappointed, but not discouraged, Miranda followed again; and the little play was repeated, with slight variation, till her great eyes were full of blinding tears, and she was ready to drop with weariness. Then the malicious cat, tired of the game and no longer curious about the ribbon, vanished altogether; and Miranda sat down to cry.

But she was not a child to make much fuss over a small disappointment. In a very few minutes she jumped up, dried her eyes with the backs of her tiny fists, and started, as she thought, straight for home. At first she ran, thinking her mother might be troubled at her absence. But not coming to the open as soon as she expected, she stopped, looked about her very carefully, and then walked forward with continual circumspection. She walked on, and on, till she knew she had gone far enough to reach home five times over. Her feet faltered, and then she stood quite still, helplessly. She knew that she was lost. All at once the ancient wood, the wood she had longed for, the wood whose darkness she had never feared, became lonely, menacing, terrible. She broke into loud wailing.

This is what Kroof had heard and was coming to investigate. But other ears heard it, too.

A tawny form, many times larger than the perfidious brown cat, but not altogether unlike it in shape, crept stealthily toward the sound. Though his limbs looked heavy, his paws large in comparison with his lank body and small, flat, cruel head, his movements nevertheless were noiseless as light. At each low-stooping, sinuous step, his tail twitched nervously. When he caught sight of the crying child he stopped, and then crept up more stealthily than before, crouching so low that his belly almost touched the ground, his neck stretched out in line with his tail.

He made absolutely no sound, yet something within Miranda's sensitive brain heard him, before he was quite within springing distance. She stopped her crying, glanced suddenly around, and fixed a darkly clear look upon his glaring green eyes. Poor little frightened and lonely child though she was, there was yet something subtly disturbing to the beast in that steady gaze of hers. It was the empty gloom, the state of being lost, which had made Miranda's fear. Of an animal, however fierce, she had no instinctive terror; and now, though she knew that the cruel-eyed beast before her was the panther, it was a sort of indignant curiosity that was uppermost in her mind.

The beast shifted his eyes uneasily under her unwavering look. He experienced a moment's indecision as to whether or not it was well, after all, to meddle with this unterrified, clear-gazing creature. Then an anger grew within him. He fixed his hypnotizing stare more resolutely, and lashed his tail with angry jerks. He was working himself up to the final and fatal spring, while Miranda watched him.

Just then a strange thing happened. Out from behind a boulder, whence she had been eying the situation, shambled the huge black form of Kroof. She was at Miranda's side in an instant; and rising upon her hind quarters, a towering, indomitable bulk, she squealed defiance to the panther. As soon as Miranda saw her "great big dog," — which she knew quite well, however, to be a bear, — she seemed to realize how frightened she had been of the panther; and she recognized that strong defence had come. With a convulsive sob she sprang and hid her tear-stained little face in the bear's shaggy flank, clutching at the soft fur with both hands. To this impetuous embrace Kroof paid no attention, but continued to glower menacingly at the panther.

As for the panther, he was unaffectedly astonished. He lost his stealthy, crouching, concentrated attitude, and rose to his full height; lifted his head, dropped his tail, and stared at the phenomenon. If this child was a protégée of Kroof's, he wanted none of her; for it would be a day of famine indeed when he would wish to force conclusions with the giant she-bear. Moreover, he recognized some sort of power and prerogative in Miranda herself, some right of sovereignty, as it were, which had made it distinctly hard for him to attack her even while she had no other defence than her disconcerting gaze. Now, however, he saw clearly that there was something very mysterious indeed about her. He decided that it would be well to have an understanding with his mate — who was more savage though less powerful than himself — that the child should not be meddled with, no matter what chance should arise. With this conclusion he wheeled about, and walked off indifferently, moving with head erect and a casual air. One would hardly have known him for the stealthy monster of five minutes before.

When he was gone Kroof lay down on her side and gently coaxed Miranda against her body. Her bereaved heart went out to the child. Her swollen teats, too, were hotly aching, and she had a kind of hope that Miranda would ease that hurt. But this, of course, never came within scope of the child's remotest idea. In every other respect, however, she showed herself most appreciative of Kroof's attentions, stroking her with light little hands, and murmuring to her much musical endearment, to which Kroof lent earnest ear. Then, laying her head on the fine fur of the bear's belly, she suddenly went fast asleep, being wearied by her wanderings and her emotions.

Late in the afternoon, toward milking-time, Kirstie aroused herself. She sat up with a startled air in her bunk in the corner of the cabin. Through the window came the rays of the westering sun. She felt troubled at having been so long asleep. And where could Miranda be? She arose, tottering for a moment, but soon found herself steady; and then she realized that she had slept off a sickness. She went to the door. The hens were diligently scratching in the dust, and Saunders eyed her with tolerance. At the fence beyond the barn the black-and-white cow lowed for the milking; and from her tether at the other side of the buckwheat field, Michael, the calf, bleated for her supper of milk and hay tea. But Miranda was nowhere to be seen.

"Miranda!" she called. And then louder,—and yet louder,—and at last with a piercing wail of anguish, as it burst upon her that Miranda was gone. The sunlit clearing, the grey cabin, the dark forest edges, all seemed to whirl and swim about her for an instant. It was only for an instant. Then she snatched up the axe from the chopping log, and with a sure instinct darted into that tongue of fir woods just behind the house.

Straight ahead she plunged, as if following a plain trail; though in truth she was little learned in woodcraft, and by her mere eyes could scarce have tracked an elephant. But her heart was clutched by a grip of ice, and she went as one tranced. All at once, however, over the mossy crest of a rock, she saw a sight which brought her to a standstill. Her eyes and her mouth opened wide in sheer amazement. Then the terrible tension relaxed. A strong shudder passed through her, and she was her steadfast self again. A smile broke up the sober lines of her face.

"Sure enough," she muttered; "the child was right. She knows a sight more about the beasts than I do."

And this is what she saw. Through the hoary arcades of the firwood walked a huge black bear, with none other than Miranda trotting by its side, and playfully stroking its rich coat. The great animal would pause from time to time, merely to nuzzle at the child with its snout or lick her hand with its narrow red tongue; but the course it was making was straight for the cabin. Kirstie stood motionless for some minutes, watching the strange scene; then, stepping out from her shelter, she hastened after them. So engrossed were they with each other that she came up undiscovered to within some twenty paces of them. Then she called out:—

"Miranda, where *have* you been?"

The child stopped, looked around, but still clung to Kroof's fur.

"Oh, mother!" she cried, eager and breathless, and trying to tell everything at once, "I was all lost—and I was just going to be eaten up—and the dear, good, big bear came and frightened the panther away—and we were just going home—and *do* come and speak to the dear, lovely, big bear! Oh, don't let it go away! *don't* let it!"

But on this point Kroof had her own views. It was Miranda she had adopted, not Kirstie; and she felt a kind of jealousy of Miranda's mother. Even while Miranda was speaking, the bear swung aside and brisklv shambled off, leaving the child half in tears.

It was a thrilling story which Miranda had to tell her mother that evening, while the black-and-white cow was getting milked, and while Michael, the calf, was having its supper of milk and hay tea. It made a profound impression on Kirstie's quick and tolerant mind. She at once realized the value to Miranda of such an affection as Kroof's. Most mothers would have been crazed with foolish fear at the situation, but Kirstie Craig was of no such weak stuff. She saw in it only a strong shield for Miranda against the gravest perils of the wood.

Chapter VII

The Intimates

AFTER this experience Miranda felt herself initiated, as she had so longed to be, into the full fellowship of the folk of the ancient wood. Almost every day Kroof came prowling about the edges of the clearing. Miranda was sure to catch sight of her before long and run to her with joyous caresses. Farther than a few steps into the open the big bear would not come, having no desire to cultivate Kirstie, or the cabin, or the cattle, or aught that appertained to civilization. But Kirstie, after watching from a courteous distance a few of these strange interviews, wisely gave the child a little more latitude. Miranda was permitted to go a certain fixed distance into the wood, but never so far as quite to lose sight of the cabin; and this permission was only for such times as she was with Kroof. Kirstie knew something about wild animals; and she knew that the black bear, when it formed an attachment, was inalienably and uncalculatingly loyal to it.

As sometimes happens in an affection which runs counter to the lines of kinship, Kroof seemed more passionately devoted to the child than she had been to her own cub. She would gaze with eyes of rapture, her mouth hanging half open in foolish fondness, while Miranda, playing about her, acquired innumerable secrets of forest-lore. Whatsoever Miranda wanted her to do, she would strive to do, as soon as she could make out what it was; for, in truth, Miranda's speech, though very pleasant to her ear, was not very intelligible to her brain. On one point, however, she was inflexible. Perhaps for a distance of thrice her own length she would follow Miranda out into the clearing, but farther than that she would not go. Persuasions, petulance, argument, tears — Miranda tried them all, but in vain. When Miranda tried going behind and pushing, or going in front and pulling, the beast liked it, and her eyes would blink humorously. But her mind was made up. This obstinacy, so disappointing to Miranda, met with Kirstie's unqualified but unexpressed approval. She did not want Kroof's ponderous bulk hanging about the house or loafing around and getting in the way when she was at work in the fields.

Though Kroof was averse to civilization, she was at the same time sagacious enough to see that she could not have Miranda always with her in the woods. She knew very well that the tall woman with red on her head was a very superior and mysterious kind of animal, — and that Miranda was her cub, — a most superior kind of cub, and always to be regarded with a secret awe, but still a cub, and belonging to the tall woman. Therefore she was not aggrieved when she found that she could not have Miranda with her in the woods for more than an hour or two at a time. In that hour or two, however, much could be done; and Kroof tried to teach Miranda many things which it is held good to know among the folk of the ancient wood. She would sniff at the mould and dig up sweet-smelling roots; and Miranda, observing the stems and leaves of them, soon came to know all the edible roots of the neighbourhood. Kroof showed her, also, the delicate dewberry, the hauntingly delicious capillaire, hidden under its trailing vines, the insipidly sweet Indian pear, and the harmless but rather cotton-woolly partridge-berry; and she taught her to shun the tempting purple fruit of the trillium, as well as the deadly snake-berry. The blueberry, dear alike to bears and men, did not grow in the heavy-timbered forest, but Miranda had known that fruit well from those earliest days in the Settlement, when she had so often stained her mouth with blueberry pie. As for the scarlet clusters of the pigeon-berry, carpeting the hillocks of the pasture, Miranda needed no teaching from Kroof to know that these were good. Then, there were all sorts of forest fungi, of many shapes and colours, —

white, pink, delicate yellow, shining orange covered with warts, creamy drab, streaky green, and even strong crimson. Toadstools, Miranda called them at first, with indiscriminating dread and aversion. But Kroof taught her better. Some, indeed, the red ones and the warty ones in particular, the wise animal would dash to pieces with her paw; and these Miranda understood to be bad. In fact, their very appearance had something ominous in it, and to Miranda's eye they had *poison* written all over them in big letters. But there was one very white and dainty-looking, sweet-smelling fungus which she would have sworn to as virtuous. As soon as she saw it, she thought of a peculiarly shy mushroom (she loved mushrooms), and ran to pick it up in triumph. But Kroof thrust her aside with such rudeness that she fell over a stump, much offended. Her indignation died away, however, as she saw Kroof tearing and stamping the pale mushrooms to minutest fragments, with every mark of loathing. From this Miranda gathered that the beautiful toadstool was a very monster of crime. It was, indeed; for it was none other than the deadly amanita, one small morsel of which would have hushed Miranda into the sleep which does not wake.

Though Miranda was safe under Kroof's tutelage, it was perhaps just as well for her at that period of her youth that she was forbidden to stray from the clearing. For there was, indeed, one tribe among the folk of the wood against whose anger Kroof's protection would have very little availed. Had Miranda gone roaming, she and Kroof, they might have found a bee tree. It is doubtful if Kroof's sagacity would have told her that Miranda's skin was not adequate to an enterprise against bee trees. The zealous bear would have probably wanted honey for the child, and the result would have been such as to shake Kirstie's confidence in Kroof's judgment.

There were, however, several well-inhabited ant-logs in that narrow circuit which Miranda was allowed to tread, and on a certain afternoon Kroof discovered one of these. She was much pleased. Here was a chance to show Miranda something very nice and very good for her health. Having attracted the child's attention, she ripped the rotten log to its heart, and began licking up the swarming insects and plump white larvæ together. Here was a treat; but the incomprehensible Miranda, with a shuddering scream, ran away. Kroof was bewildered. She finished the ants, however, while she was about it. Whereafter she was called upon to hear a long lecture from Miranda, to the effect that ants were not good to eat, and that it was very cruel to tear open their nests and steal their eggs. Of course, as Kroof did not at all understand what she was driving at, there was no room for an argument; which, considering the points involved, is much to be regretted.

Though Miranda had now, so to speak, the freedom of the wood, she was not really intimate with any of the furtive folk, saving only, of course, the irrepressible squirrels who lived in the cabin roof. She saw the wild creatures now very close at hand, and they went about their business under her eye without concern. They realized that it was no use trying with her their game of invisibility. No matter how perfect their stillness, no matter how absolutely they made themselves one with their surroundings, they felt her clear, unwavering, friendly eyes look them through and through. This was at first a troubling mystery to them. Who was this youngling, — for youth betrays itself even to the most primitive perceptions, — who, for all her youth, set their traditions and elaborate devices so easily at naught? Their instincts told them, however, that she was no foe to the weakest of them; and so they let her see them at their affairs unabashed, though avoiding her with a kind of careful awe.

Kroof, too, they all avoided, but with a difference. They knew that she was not averse to an occasional meal of flesh meat, but that she would not greatly trouble herself in pursuit of it. All they had to do, these lesser folk of the wood, was to keep at a safe distance from the sweep of her mighty paw, and they felt at ease in her neighbourhood. All but the hare — *he* knew that Kroof considered him and his long-eared children a special delicacy, well worth the effort of a bear. Miranda wondered why she could never see anything of the hare when she was out with Kroof. She did see him sometimes, indeed; but always at a distance, and for an instant only. On these occasions, Kroof did not see him at all; and Miranda soon came to realize that she could see more clearly than even the furtive folk themselves. They could hide themselves from each other by stillness and by self-effacement; but Miranda's eyes always inexorably distinguished the ruddy fox from the yellow-brown, rotten log on which he flattened himself. She instantly differentiated the moveless nuthatch from the knot on the trunk, the squatting grouse from the lichened stone, the wood-mouse from the curled brown leaf, the crouching wild-cat from the mottled branch. Consequently the furtive folk gradually began to pay her the tribute of ignoring her, which meant that they trusted her to let them alone. They kept their reserve; but under her interested scrutiny the nut-hatch would walk up the rough-barked pine trunk and pick insects out from under the grey scales; the golden-winged wood-pecker would hunt down the fat, white grubs which he delighted in, and hammer sharply on the dead wood a few feet above her head; the slim, brown stoat would chase beetles among the tree roots, un-troubled by her discreet proximity; the beruffed cock-grouse would drum from the top of his stump till the air was full of the soft thunder of his vauntings, and his half-grown brood would dust them-selves in the deserted ant-hill in the sun-niest corner of the clearing. Only the pair of crows which, seeing great oppor-tunities about the reoccupied clearing, had taken up their dwelling in the top of a tall spruce close behind the cabin, held suspiciously aloof from Miranda. They often talked her over, in harsh tones that jarred the ancient stillness; and they considered her intimacy with Kroof altogether contrary to the order of things. Being themselves exemplars of duplicity, they were quite convinced that Miranda had ulterior motives, too deep for them to fathom; and they therefore respected her immensely. But they did not trust her, of course. The shy rain-birds, however, trusted her, and would whistle to each other their long, melancholy calls foretelling rain, even though she were standing within a few steps of them, and staring at them with all her might; and this was a most unheard-of favour on the part of the rain-birds, who are too reticent to let themselves be heard when any one is near enough to see them. There might be three or four uttering their slow, inexpressibly pathetic cadences all around the clearing; but Kirstie could never catch a glimpse of them, though many a time she listened with deep longing in her heart as their remote voices thrilled across the dewy oncoming of the dusk.

Miranda saw the panther only once

again that year. It was about a month after her meeting with Kroof. She was alone, just upon the edge of the buckwheat field, and peering into the shadowy, transparent stillness to see what she could see. What she saw sent her little heart straight up into her mouth. There, not a dozen paces from her, lying flat along a fallen tree, was the panther. He was staring at her, with his eyes half shut. Startled though she was, Miranda's experience with Kroof had made her very self-confident. She stood moveless, staring back into those dangerous, half-shut eyes. After a moment or two the beautiful beast arose and stretched himself with great deliberation, reaching out and digging in his claws, as an ordinary cat does when it stretches. At the same time he yawned prodigiously, so that it seemed to Miranda he would surely split to his ears, and she looked right into his great pink throat. Then he stepped lightly down from the tree, — on the side farthest from Miranda, — and walked away with the air of not wishing to intrude.

This same summer, too, so momentous in its events, Miranda first met Wapiti, the delicate-antlered buck, and Ganner, the big Canada lynx. Needless to say, they were not in company. One morning, as she sat in a fence corner, absorbed in building a little house of twigs around a sick butterfly, she heard a loud snort just at her elbow. Much startled, she gave a little cry as she looked up, and something jumped back from the fence. She saw a bright brown head, crowned with splendid, many-pronged antlers, and a pair of large, liquid eyes looking at her with mild wonder.

"Oh, you *be-autiful* deer, did I frighten you?" she cried, knowing the visitor by pictures she had seen; and she poked her little hand through the fence in greeting. The buck seemed very curious about the scarlet ribbon at her neck, and eyed it steadily for half a minute. Then he came close up to the fence again, and sniffed her hand with his fine black nostrils, opening and closing them sensitively. He let her stroke his smooth muzzle, and held his head quite still under the caressing of her hand. Then some unusual sound caught his ear. It was Kirstie hoeing potatoes near by; and presently the furrow she was following brought her into view behind the corner of the barn. The scarlet kerchief on her hair flamed hotly in the sun. The buck raised his head high, and stared, and finally seemed to decide that the apparition was a hostile one. With a snort, and an impatient stamp of his polished hoof, he wheeled about and trotted off into the wood.

Her introduction to Ganner, the lynx, was under less gracious auspices.

Michael, the calf, who had been growing excellently all summer, was kept tethered during the daytime to a stake in a corner of the wild-grass meadow, about fifty yards from the edge of the forest. A little nearer the cabin was a long thicket of blackberry brakes and elder bushes and wild clematis, forming a dense tangle, in which Miranda had, with great pains and at the cost of terrific scratches, formed herself a delectable hiding-place.

Here she would play house, and sometimes take a nap, in the hot mornings, while her mother would be at work acres away, at the very opposite side of the clearing.

One day, about eleven in the morning, Michael was lying at the limit of her tether nearest the cabin, when she saw a strange beast come out of the forest and halt to look at her. The animal was of a greyish rusty brown, very pale on the belly and neck, and nearly as tall as Michael herself; but its body was curiously short in proportion to the length of its powerful legs. It had a perfectly round face, with round glaring eyes, long stiff black tufts on the tips of its sharp-pointed ears, and a fierce-looking, whitish brown whisker brushed away, as it were, from under its chin. Its tail was a mere thick, brown stump of a tail, looking as if it had been chopped off short. The creature gazed all around, warily; then crouched low, its hind quarters rather higher in the air than its fore shoulders, and stepping softly, came straight for Michael.

Inexperienced as Michael was, she knew that this was nothing less than death itself approaching her. She sprang up, her awkward legs spread wide apart, her whole weight straining on the tether, her eyes, rolling white, fixed in horror on the dreadful object. From her throat came a long, shrill bleat of appeal and despair.

There was no mistaking that cry. It brought Miranda from her playhouse in an instant. In the next instant she took in the situation. "Mother! *Mothe-e-er!*" she screamed at the top of her voice, and flew to the defence of her beloved Michael.

The lynx, at this unexpected interference, stopped short. Miranda did not look formidable, and he was not alarmed by any means. But she looked unusual, — and that bit of bright red at her throat might mean something which he did not understand, — and there was something not quite natural, something to give him pause, in a youngster displaying this reckless courage. For a second or two, therefore, he sat straight up like a cat, considering; and his tufted ears the while, very erect, with the strange whiskers under his chin, gave him an air that was fiercely dignified. His hesitation, however, was but for a moment. Satisfied that Miranda did not count, he came on again, more swiftly; and Miranda, seeing that she had failed to frighten him away, just flung her arms around Michael's neck and screamed.

The scream should have reached Kirstie's ear across the whole breadth of the clearing; but a flaw of wind carried it away, and the cabin intervened to dull its edge. Other ears than Kirstie's, however, heard it; heard, too, and understood Michael's bleating. The black-and-white cow was far away, in another pasture. (Kirstie saw her running frantically up and down along the fence, and thought the flies were tormenting her.) But just behind the thicket lay the two steers, Bright and Star, contemplatively chewing their midday cud. Both had risen heavily to their feet at Michael's first appeal. As Miranda's scream rang out, Bright's sorrel head appeared around the corner of the thicket, anxious to investigate. He stopped at sight of Ganner, held his muzzle high in air, snorted loudly, and shook his head with a great show of valour. Immediately after him came Star, the black-and-white brindle. But of a different temper was he. The moment his eyes fell upon Michael's foe and Miranda's, down went his long, straight horns, up went his brindled tail, and with a bellow of rage he charged.

The gaunt steer was an antagonist whom Ganner had no stomach to face. With an angry snarl, which showed Miranda a terrifying set of white teeth in a very red mouth, he turned his stump of a tail, laid flat his tufted ears, and made for the forest with long, splendid leaps, his exaggerated hind legs seeming to volley him forward like a ball. In about five seconds he was out of sight among the trees; and Star, snorting and switching his tail, stood pawing the turf haughtily in front of Miranda and Michael.

It was Miranda who named the big lynx "Ganner" that day; because, as she told her mother afterward, that was what he said when Star came and drove him away.

Chapter VIII

Axe and Antler

THE next winter went by in the main much like the former one. But more birds came to be fed as the season advanced, because Miranda's fame had gone abroad amongst them. The snow was not so deep, the cold not so severe. No panther came again to claw at their roof by night. But there were certain events which made the season stand out sharply from all others in the eyes of both Kirstie and Miranda.

Throughout December and January Wapiti, the buck, with two slim does accompanying him, would come and hang about the barn for several days at a time, nibbling at the scattered straw. With the two steers, Star and Bright, Wapiti was not on very good terms. They would sometimes thrust at him resentfully, whereupon he would jump aside, as if on springs, stamp twice sharply with his polished fore hoofs, and level at them the fourteen threatening spear points of his antlers. But the challenge never came to anything. As for the black-and-white cow, she seemed to admire Wapiti greatly, though he met her admiration with the most lofty indifference. One day Miranda let him and the two does lick some coarse salt out of a dish, after which enchanting experience all three would follow her straight up to the cabin door. They even took to following Kirstie about, which pleased and flattered her more than she would acknowledge to Miranda, and earned them many a cold buckwheat pancake. To them the cold pancakes, though leathery and tough, were a tit-bit of delight; but along in January they tore themselves away from such raptures and removed to other feeding grounds.

Toward spring, to Miranda's great delight, she made acquaintance with Ten-Tine, the splendid bull caribou whom she had just seen the winter before. He and his antlered cows were migrating southward by slow stages. They were getting tired of the dry moss and lichen of the barrens which lay a week's journey northward from the clearing. They began to crave the young shoots of willow and poplar that would now be bursting with sap along the more southerly streams. Looking from the window one morning, before the cattle had been let out, Miranda saw Ten-Tine emerge from the woods and start with long, swinging strides across the open. His curiously flattened, leaf-like antlers lay back on a level with his shoulders, and his nose pointed straight before him. The position was just the one to enable him to go through the woods without getting his horns entangled. From the middle of his forehead projected, at right angles to the rest of the antlers, two broad, flat, palmated prongs, a curious enlargement of the central ones. His cows, whose antlers were little less splendid than his own, but lacking in the frontal projection, followed at his heels. In colour he was of a very light, whitish-drab, quite unlike the warm brown of Wapiti's coat.

In passing the barn Ten-Tine caught sight of some tempting fodder, and stopped to try it. Kirstie's straw proved very much to the taste of the whole herd. While they were feeding delightedly, Miranda stole out to make friends with them. She took, as a tribute, a few handfuls of the hens' buckwheat, in a bright yellow bowl. As she approached, Ten-Tine lifted his fine head and eyed her curiously. Had it been the rutting season, he would no doubt have straightway challenged her to mortal combat. But now, unless he saw a wolf, a panther, or a lynx, he was good-tempered and inquisitive. This small creature looked harmless, and there was undoubtedly something quite remarkable about her. What was that shining thing which she held out in front of her? And what was that other very bright thing around her neck? He stopped feeding, and watched her intently, his head held in an attitude of indecision, just a little lower than his shoulders. The cows took a look also, and felt curious, but were concerned rather to satisfy their hunger than their curiosity. They left the matter easily to Ten-Tine.

Miranda had learned many things already from her year among the folk of the wood. One of these things was that all the furtive folk dreaded and resented rough movement. Their manners were always beyond reproach. The fiercest of them moved ever with an aristocratic grace and poise. They knew the difference between swiftness and haste. All abruptness they abhorred. In lines of beauty they eluded their enemies. They killed in curves.

She did not, therefore, attempt to go straight up and take Ten-Tine's acquaintance by storm. She paused discreetly some dozen steps away, held out the dish to him, and murmured her inarticulate, soft persuasions. Not being versed in the caribou tongue, she trusted the tones of her voice to reveal her good intention.

Seeing that she would come no nearer, Ten-Tine's curiosity refused to be balked.

But he was dubious, very dubious. Like Wapiti, he stamped when he was in doubt; but the hoofs he stamped with were much larger, broader, clumsier, less polished than Wapiti's, being formed for running over such soft surfaces as bogland and snow insufficiently packed, where Wapiti's trim feet would cut through like knives.

Step by step he drew nearer. There was something in Miranda's clear gaze that gave him confidence. At length he was near enough to touch the yellow bowl with his flexible upper lip. He saw that the bowl contained something. He extended his muzzle over the rim, and, to Miranda's surprise, blew into it. The grain flew in every direction, some of it sticking to his own moist lips. He drew back, a little startled. Then he licked his lips; and he liked the taste. Back went his muzzle into the interesting bowl; and, after sniffing again very gently, he licked up the whole contents.

"Oh, greedy!" exclaimed Miranda, in tender rebuke, and started back to the cabin to get him some more.

"Wouldn't Saunders be cross," she thought to herself, "if he knew I was giving his buckwheat to the nice deer?"

Ten-Tine followed close behind her, sniffing inquisitively at the red ribbon on her neck. When Miranda went in for the buckwheat, he tried to enter with her, but his antlers had too much spread for the doorway. Kirstie, who was busy sweeping, looked up in amazement as the great head darkened her door.

"Drat the child!" she exclaimed; "she'll be bringing all the beasts of the wood in to live with us before long."

She did not grudge Ten-Tine the few handfuls of buckwheat, however, though he blew half of it over the floor so that she had to sweep it up. When he had finished, and perceived that no more was forthcoming, he backed off reluctantly from the door and began smelling around the window-sill, pushing his curious nose tentatively against the glass.

Now it chanced that all the way down from the barrens Ten-Tine and his little herd had been hungrily pursued, although they did not know it. Four of the great grey timber wolves were on their track. Savage but prudent, the wolves were unwilling to attack the herd, for they knew the caribou's fighting prowess. But they awaited a chance to cut off one of the cows and hunt her down alone. For days they had kept the trail, faring very scantly by the way; and now they were both ravenous and enraged. Emerging from the woods, they saw the five cows at feed by the barn, with Ten-Tine nowhere in sight. The opportunity was too rare a one to miss. They seized it. All four gaunt forms abreast, they came galloping across the snow in silence, their long, grey snouts wrinkled, their white fangs uncovered, their grey-and-white shoulders rising and falling in unison, their cloudy tails floating straight out behind them.

Just in time the cows saw them coming. There was a half second of motionless consternation. Then nimbly they sprang into a circle, hind quarters bunched together, levelled antlers all pointing outward. It was the accurate inherited discipline of generations.

Without a sound, save a deep, gasping breath, the wolves made their leap, striving to clear that bayonet hedge of horns. Two were hurled back, yelping. One brought a cow to her knees, half clear of the circle, his fangs in her neck, and would have finished her but that her next neighbour prodded him so fiercely in the flank that he let go with a shrill snarl. But the fourth wolf found the weak point in the circle. The foolish young cow upon whom he sprang went wild at once with fright. She broke from the ring and fled. The next instant the wolf was at her throat.

The moment he pulled her down the other wolves sprang upon her. The rest of the cows, maintaining their position of defence, viewed her plight with considerable unconcern, doubtless holding that her folly was well served, and that she was worth no better end. But Ten-Tine, who had suddenly taken in the situation, had other views about it. To him the foolish young cow was most important. With a shrill note of rage, half bleat, half bellow, he charged down to the rescue

The first wolf he struck was hurled against the corner of the barn, and came limping back to the fray with no great enthusiasm. Upon the next he came down with both front feet, fairly breaking the creature's back. Instantly the other two fastened upon his flanks, trying to pull him down; while he, bounding and rearing, strove heroically to shake them off in order to reach them with horns and hoofs. The bleeding cow, meanwhile, struggled to her feet and took refuge within the dauntless circle, which rather grudgingly opened to admit her. For this they must not be judged too harshly; for in caribou eyes she had committed the crime of crimes in breaking ranks and exposing the whole herd to destruction.

At this stage in the encounter the valiant Ten-Tine found himself in desperate straits; but help came from an unexpected quarter. The factor which the wolves had not allowed for was Kirstie Craig. At the first sight of them Kirstie had been filled with silent rage. She had believed that wolves were quite extinct throughout all the neighbouring forests; and now in their return she saw a perpetual menace. But at least they were scarce, she knew that; and on the instant she resolved that this little pack should meet no milder fate than extermination.

"It's wolves! Don't you stir outside this door!" she commanded grimly, in that voice which Miranda never dreamed of disobeying. Miranda, trembling with excitement, her eyes wide and her cheeks white, climbed to the window, and flattened her face against it. Kirstie rushed out, slamming the door.

As she passed the chopping-block, Kirstie snatched up her axe. Her fine face was set like iron. The black eyes blazed fury. It was a desperate venture, to attack three maddened wolves, with no ally to support her save a caribou bull; but Kirstie, as we have seen, was not a woman for half measures.

The first sweep of that poised and practised axe caught the nearest wolf just behind the fore quarters, and almost shore him in two. Thus suddenly freed on one side, Ten-Tine wheeled like lightning to catch his other assailant, but the animal sprang back. In evading Ten-Tine's horns, he almost fell over Kirstie, who, thus balked of her full deadly swing, just managed to fetch him a short stroke under the jaw with the flat of the blade. It was enough, however, to fell him for an instant, and that instant was enough for Ten-Tine. Bounding into the air, the big caribou came down with both sharp fore hoofs, like chisels, squarely on the middle of his adversary's ribs. The stroke was slaughterously decisive. Ribs of steel could not have endured it, and in a very few seconds the shape of bloody grey fur upon the snow bore scant resemblance to a wolf.

The last of the pack, who had been lamed by Ten-Tine's onslaught, had prudently drawn off when he saw Kirstie coming. Now he turned tail. Kirstie, determined that not one should escape, gave chase. She could run as can few women. She was bent on her grim purpose of extermination. At first the wolf's lameness hindered him; but just as he was about to turn at bay and fight dumbly to the death, after the manner of his kind, the effort which he had been making loosened the strained muscles, and he found his pace. Stretching himself out on his long gallop, he shot away from his pursuer as if she had been standing still.

Kirstie stopped, swung her axe, and hurled it after him with all her strength. It struck the mark. Had it struck true, edge on, it would have fulfilled her utmost intention; but it struck, with the thick of the head, squarely upon the brute's rump. The blow sent him rolling end over end across the snow. He yelped with astonishment and terror; but recovering himself again in a second, he went bounding like a grey ball of fur over a brush heap, and vanished down the forest arches.

When Kirstie turned round she saw Miranda, white, pitiful, and bewildered, in the doorway; while Ten-Tine and his cows, without waiting to thank her, were trotting away across the white fields, their muzzles thrust far forward, their antlers laid along their backs. From Ten-Tine himself, and from the wounded young cow, the blood dripped scarlet and steaming at every stride.

Chapter IX

The Pax Mirandæ

AFTER this experience, Kirstie would have been more anxious than before about Miranda, had it not been for the child's remarkable friendship with the great she-bear. As soon as the snow was gone, and the ancient wood again began to lure Miranda with its mystic stillness and transparent twilight, Kroof reappeared, as devoted as ever. When Kroof was absent, the woods were to the child a forbidden realm, into which she could only peer with longing and watch the furtive folk with those initiated eyes of hers.

A little later when the mosses were dry, and when the ground was well heartened with the fecundating heats of June, Miranda had further proof of her peculiar powers of vision. One day she and

Kroof came upon a partridge hen with her new-hatched brood, at the edge of a thicket of young birches. The hen went flopping and fluttering off among the trees, as if sorely wounded; and Kroof, convinced of a speedy capture, followed eagerly. She gave a glance about her first, however, to see if there were any partridge chicks in the neighbourhood. To Miranda's astonishment, the wise animal saw none. But Miranda saw them distinctly. There they were all about her, moveless little brown balls, exactly like the leaves and the moss and the scattered things of the forest floor. Some were half hidden under a leaf or twig; some squatted in the open, just in the positions in which the alarm had found them. They shut their eyes even, to make themselves more at one with their surroundings. They would have endured any fate, they would have died on the spot, rather than move, so perfect was their baby obedience to the partridge law. This obedience had its reward. It gave them invisibility to all the folk of the wood, friends and foes alike. But there was no such thing as deceiving Miranda's eyes. She was not concerned about the mother partridge, because she saw through her pretty trick and knew that Kroof could never catch her. Indeed, in her innocence she did not think good Kroof would hurt her if she did catch her. But these moveless chicks, on the other hand, were interesting. One — two — three — Miranda counted ten of them, and there were more about somewhere, she imagined. Presently the mother bird came flopping around in a circle, to see how things were going. She saw Miranda stoop and pick up one of the precious brown balls, and then another, curiously but gently. In her astonishment the distracted bird forgot Kroof for a second, and was almost caught. Escaping this peril by a sudden wild dash, and realizing that from Miranda there was no concealment, she flew straight into the densest part of the thicket and gave a peremptory call. At the sound each little motionless ball came to life. The two that were lying as if dead on Miranda's outstretched palms hopped to the ground; and all darted into the thicket. A few low but sharply articulated clucks, and the mother bird led her brood off swiftly through the bush; while Kroof, somewhat crestfallen, came shambling back to Miranda.

All this time, in spite of the affair of the wolves, the attack of Ganner, the lynx, on Michael, and that tell-tale spot of blood and fur on the snow, where the owl had torn the hare for his midnight feast, Miranda had regarded the folk of the ancient wood as a gentle people, living for the most part in a voiceless amity. Her seeing eyes quite failed to see the unceasing tragedy of the stillness. She did not guess that the furtive folk, whom she watched about their business, went always with fear at their side and death lying in wait at every turn. She little dreamed that, for most of them, the very price of life itself was the ceaseless extinguishing of life.

It was during the summer that Miranda found her first and only flaw in Kroof's perfections; for Kroof she regarded as second only to her mother among created beings. But on one memorable day, when she ran across the fields to meet Kroof at the edge of the wood, the great bear was too much occupied to come forward as usual. She was sniffing at something on the ground which she held securely under one of her huge paws. Miranda ran forward to see what it was.

To her horror it was the warm and bleeding body of a hare.

She shrank back, sickened at the sight. Then, in flaming indignation she struck Kroof again and again in the face with the palms of her little hands. Kroof was astonished, — temperately astonished, — for she always knew Miranda was peculiar. She lifted her snout high in the air to escape the blows, shut her eyes, and meekly withdrew the offending paw.

"Oh, Kroof, how *could* you! I hate you, bad Kroof! You are just like the wolves!" cried Miranda, her little bosom bursting with wrath and tears. Kroof understood that she was in grievous disgrace. Carrying the dead hare with her, Miranda ran out into the potato patch, fetched the hoe, returned to the spot where the bear still sat in penitential contemplation, and proceeded in condemnatory silence to dig a hole right under Kroof's nose. Here she buried the hare, tenderly smoothing the ground above it. Then throwing the hoe down violently, she flung her arms about Kroof's neck, and burst into a passion of tears.

"How *could* you do it, Kroof?" she sobbed. "Oh, perhaps you'll be wanting to eat up Miranda some day!"

Kroof suffered herself to be led away from the unhappy spot. Soon Miranda grew calm, and the painful scene seemed forgotten. The rest of the afternoon was spent very pleasantly in eating wild raspberries along the farther side of the clearing. To Kroof's mind it gradually became clear that her offence lay in killing the hare; and as it was obvious that Miranda liked hares, she resolved never to offend again in this respect, at least while Miranda was anywhere in the neighbourhood

After Miranda had gone home, however, the philosophical Kroof strolled back discreetly to where the hare was buried. She dug it up, and ate it with great satisfaction, and afterward she smoothed down the earth again, that Miranda might not know.

After this trying episode Miranda had every reason to believe that Kroof's reformation was complete. Little by little, as month followed month, and season followed season, and year rolled into year at the quiet cabin in the clearing, Miranda forgot the few scenes of blood which had been thrust upon her. The years now little varied one from another; yet to Miranda the life was not monotonous. Each season was for her full of events, full of tranquil uneventfulness for Kirstie. The cabin became more homelike as currant and lilac bushes grew up around it, a green, sweet covert for birds, and abundant scarlet-blossomed bean-vines mantled the barrenness of its weathered logs. The clearing prospered. The stock increased. Old Dave hardly ever visited at the clearing but he went back laden with stuff to sell for Kirstie at the Settlement. Among the folk of the forest Miranda's ascendency kept on growing, little by little, till, though none of the beasts came to know her as Kroof did, they all had a tendency to follow her at respectful distance, without seeming to do so. They never killed in her presence, so that a perpetual truce, as it were, came at last to rule within eyeshot of her inescapable gaze. Sometimes the advent of spring would bring Kroof to the clearing not alone, but with a furry and jolly black morsel of a cub at her side. The cub never detracted in the least from the devotion which she paid to Miranda. It always grew up to young bearhood in more or less amiable tolerance of its mother's incomprehensible friend, only to drift away at last to other feeding grounds; for Kroof was absolute in her own domain, and suffered not even her own offspring to trespass thereon, when once they had reached maturity. Cubs might come, and cubs might go; but the love of Kroof and Miranda was a thing that rested unchanging.

In the winters, Miranda now did most of the knitting, while Kirstie wove, on a great clacking loom, the flax which her little farm produced abundantly. They had decided not to keep sheep at the clearing, lest their presence should lure back the wolves. One warm day toward spring, when Old Dave, laden with an ample pack of mittens, stockings, and socks which Miranda's active fingers had fashioned, was slowly trudging along the trail on his way back to the Settlement, he became aware that a pair of foxes followed him. They came not very near, nor did they pay him any marked attention. They merely seemed to "favour his company," as he himself put it. He was thus curiously escorted for perhaps a mile or two, to his great bewilderment; for he knew no reason why he should be so chosen out for honour in the wood. At another time, when similarly burdened, Wapiti, the buck, came up and sniffed at him, very amicably. During the next winter, when he was carrying the same magic merchandise, several hares went leaping beside him, not very near, but as if seeking the safety of his presence. The mystery of all this weighed upon him. He was at first half inclined to think that he was "ha'nted"; but fortunately he took thought to examine the tracks, and so assured himself that his inexplicable companions were of real flesh and blood. Nevertheless, he found himself growing shy of his periodical journeyings through the wood, and at last he opened his mind to Kirstie on the subject.

Kirstie was amused in her grave way.

"Why, Dave," she explained, "didn't you know Miranda was that thick with the wild things she's half wild herself? Weren't you carrying a lot of Miranda's knit stuff when the creatures followed you?"

"That's so, Kirstie!" was the old lumberman's reply. "I recollec' as how the big buck kep' a-sniffin' at my pack of socks an' mits, too!"

"They were some of Miranda's friends; and when they smelled of those mits they thought she was somewhere around, or else they knew you must be a friend of hers."

Thenceforward Old Dave always looked for something of a procession in his honour whenever he carried Miranda's knittings to the Settlement; and he was intensely proud of the distinction. He talked about it among his gossips, of course; and therefore a lot of strange stories began to circulate. It was said by some that Kirstie and Miranda held converse with the beasts in plain English such as common mortals use, and knew all the secrets of the woods, and much besides that "humans' have no call to know. By others, more superstitious and fanatical, it was whispered that no mere animals formed the circle of Kirstie's associates, but that spirits, in the guise of hares, foxes, cats, panthers, bears, were her familiars at the solitary cabin. Such malicious tales cost Old Dave many a bitter hour, as well as more than one sharp combat, till the gossips learned to keep a bridle on their tongues when he was by. As for Young Dave, he had let the clearing and all its affairs drop from his mind, and, betaking himself to a wild region to the north of the Quah-Davic, was fast making his name as a hunter and trapper. He came but seldom to the Settlement, and when he came he had small ear for the Settlement scandals. His mind was growing large, and quiet, and tolerant, among the great solitudes.

Chapter X

The Routing of the Philistines

IN the seventh year of Kirstie's exile, something occurred which gave the Settlement gossip a fresh impulse, and added a colour of awe to the mystery which surrounded the clearing.

The winter changed to a very open one, so that long before spring Kroof awoke in her lair under the pine root. There was not enough snow to keep her warm and asleep. But the ground was frozen, food was scarce, and she soon became hungry. Miranda observed her growing leanness, and tried the experiment of bringing her a mess of boiled beans from the cabin pot. To the hungry bear the beans were a revelation. She realized that Miranda's mother was in some way connected with the experience, and her long reserve melted away in the warmth of her responsive palate. The next day, about noon, as Kirstie and Miranda were sitting down to their meal, Kroof appeared at the cabin door and sniffed longingly at the threshold.

"What's that sniffing at the door?" wondered Kirstie, with some uneasiness in her grave voice. But Miranda had flown at once to the window to look out.

"Why, mother, it's Kroof!" she cried, clapping her hands with delight, and before her mother could say a word, she had thrown the door wide open. In shambled the bear forthwith, blinking her shrewd little eyes. She seated herself on her haunches, near the table, and gazed with intent curiosity at the fire. At this moment a dry stick snapped and crackled sharply, whereupon she backed off to a safer distance, but still kept her eyes upon the strange phenomenon.

Both Kirstie and Miranda had been watching her with breathless interest, to see how she would comport herself, but now Miranda broke silence.

"Oh! you dear old Kroof, we're so

glad you've come at last to see us!" she cried, rushing over and flinging both arms around the animal's neck. Kirstie's face looked a doubtful indorsement of the welcome. Kroof paid no attention to Miranda's caresses beyond a hasty lick at her ear, and continued to study the fascinating flames. This quietness of demeanour reassured Kirstie, whose hospitality thereupon asserted itself.

"Give the poor thing some buckwheat cakes, Miranda," she said. "I'm sure she's come because she's hungry."

Miranda preferred to think the visit was due to no such interested motives; but she at once took up a plate of cakes which she had drenched in molasses for the requirements of her own taste. She set the plate on the edge of the table nearest to her visitor, and gently pulled the bear's snout down toward it. No second invitation was needed. The fire was forgotten. The enchanting smell of buckwheat cakes and molasses was a new one to Kroof's nostrils, but the taste for it was there, full grown and waiting. Out went her narrow red tongue. The cakes disappeared rather more rapidly than was consistent with good manners: the molasses was deftly licked up, and with a grin of rapture she looked about for more. Just in front of Kirstie stood a heaping dish of the dainties hot from the griddle. With an eager but tentative paw Kroof reached out for them. This was certainly not manners. Kirstie removed the dish beyond her reach, while Miranda firmly pushed the trespassing paw from the table.

"No, Kroof, you shan't have any more at all, unless you are good!" she admonished, with hortatory finger uplifted.

There are few animals so quick to take a hint as the bear, and Kroof's wits had grown peculiarly alert during her long intimacy with Miranda. She submitted with instant meekness, and waited, with tongue hanging out, while Miranda prepared her a huge bowl of bread and molasses. When she had eaten this, she investigated everything about the cabin, and finally went to sleep on a mat in the corner of the inner room. Before sundown she got up and wandered off to her lair, being still drowsy with winter sleep.

After this the old bear came daily at noon to the cabin, dined with Kirstie and Miranda, and dozed away the afternoon on her mat in the chosen corner. Kirstie came to regard her as a member of the household. To the cattle and the poultry she paid no attention whatever. In a few days the oxen ceased to lower their horns as she passed; and the cock, Saunders's equally haughty successor, refrained from the shrill expletives of warning with which he had been wont to herald her approach.

One afternoon, before spring had fairly set in, there came two unwelcome visitors to the cabin. In a lumber-camp some fifteen miles away, on a branch of the Quah-Davic, there had been trouble. Two of the "hands," surly and mutinous all winter, had at last, by some special brutality, enraged the "boss" and their mates beyond all pardon. Hooted and beaten from the camp, they had started through the woods by the shortest road to the

Settlement. Their hearts were black with pent-up fury. About three o'clock in the afternoon, they happened upon the clearing, and demanded something to eat.

Though sullen, and with a kind of menace in their air, their words were civil enough at first, and Kirstie busied herself to supply what seemed to her their just demands. The laws of hospitality are very binding in the backwoods. Miranda, meanwhile, not liking the looks of the strangers, kept silently aloof and scrutinized them.

When Kirstie had set before them a good meal, — hot tea, and hot boiled beans, and eggs, and white bread and butter, — they were disappointed because she gave them no pork, and they were not slow to demand it.

"I've got none," said Kirstie; "we don't eat pork here. You ought to get along well enough on what's good enough for Miranda and me."

For a backwoods house to be without pork, the indispensable, the universal, the lumberman's staff of life, was something unheard of. They both thought she was keeping back the pork out of meanness.

"You lie!" exclaimed one, a lean, short, swarthy ruffian. The other got up and took a step toward the woman, where she stood, dauntlessly eying them. His scrubby red beard bristled, his massive shoulders hunched themselves ominously toward his big ears.

"You git that pork, and be quick about it!" he commanded, with the addition of such phrases of emphasis as the lumberman uses, but does not use in the presence of women.

"Beast!" exclaimed Kirstie, eyes and cheeks flaming. "Get out of this house." And she glanced about for a weapon. But in a second the ruffian had seized her. Though stronger than most men, she was no match for him — a noted bully and a cunning master of the tricks of the ring. She was thrown in a second. Miranda, with a scream of rage, snatched up a table knife and darted to her mother's aid; but the shorter ruffian, now delighted with the game, shouted: "Settle the old woman,

Bill. I'll see to the gal!" and made a grab for Miranda.

It had all happened so suddenly that Kirstie was, for a moment, stunned. Then, realizing the full horror of the situation, a strength as of madness came upon her. She set her teeth into the wrist of her assailant with such fury that he yelled and for a second loosed his hold. In that second, tearing herself half free, she clutched his throat with her long and powerful fingers. It was only an instant's respite, but it was enough to divert the other scoundrel's attention from Miranda. With a huge laugh he turned to free his mate from that throttling grip.

His purpose was never fulfilled. Kroof, just at this instant, thrust her nose from the door of the inner room, half awake, and wondering at the disturbance. Her huge bulk was like a nightmare. The swarthy wretch stood for an instant spellbound in amazement. With a savage growl, Kroof launched herself at him, and he, darting around the table, wrenched the door open and fled.

The other miscreant, though well occupied with Kirstie's mad grip at his throat, had seen, from the corner of his eyes, that black monster emerge like fate and charge upon his comrade. To him, Kroof looked as big as an ox. With a gasping curse he tore himself free; and, hurling Kirstie half across the table, he rushed from the cabin. His panic was lest the monster should return and catch him, like a rat in a pit, where there was no chance of escape.

As a matter of fact, Kroof *was* just returning, with an angry realization that her foe could run faster than she could. And lo! here was another of the same breed in the very doorway before her. As she confronted him, his eyes nearly started from his head. With a yell he dodged past, nimble as a loon's neck. Savagely she struck out at him with her punishing paw. Had she caught him, there would have been one rogue the fewer, and blood on the cabin threshold. But she missed, and he went free. He ran wildly over the snow patches in pursuit of his fleeing comrade; while Kroof, all a-bristle with indignation, hurried into the cabin, to be hugged and praised with grateful tears by Kirstie and Miranda.

When the first of the fugitives, the lean and swarthy one, reached the edge of the woods, he paused to look back. There was no one following but his comrade, who came up a moment later and clutched at him, panting heavily. Neither, for a minute or two, had breath for any word but a broken curse. The big, bristly scoundrel called Bill was bleeding at the wrist from Kirstie's bite, and his throat, purple and puffed, bore witness to the strength of Kirstie's fingers. The other had got off scot free. The two stared at each other, cowed and discomfited.

"Ever see the likes o' that?" queried Bill, earnestly.

"Be damned ef 't wan't the devil himself!" asseverated his companion.

"Oh, hell! 't were jest a b'ar!" retorted Bill, in a tone of would-be derision. "But bigger'n a steer! *I* don't want none of it!"

"B'ar er devil, what's the odds? Let's git, says I!" was the response; and simultaneously the two lifted their eyes to observe the sun and get their bearings. But it was not the sun they saw. Their jaws fell. Their hair rose. For a moment they stood rooted to the ground in abject horror.

Right above their heads, crouched close upon the vast up-sloping limb of a hoary pine, lay a panther, looking down upon them with fixed, dilating stare. They saw his claws, protruding, and set firmly into the bark. They saw the backward, snarling curl of his lips as his head reached down toward them over the edge of his perch. For several choking heart-beats the picture bit itself into their coarse brains; then, with a gurgling cry that came as one voice from the two throats, both sprang aside like hares and ran wildly down the trail.

Within a few hours of their arrival at the Settlement, this was the story on all lips, — that Kirstie's cabin was guarded by familiars, who could take upon themselves at will the form of bear, panther, wolf, or mad bull moose, for the terrorizing of such travellers as might chance to trespass upon that unholy solitude. The Settlement held a few superstitious souls who believed this tale; while the rest pretended to believe it because it gave them something to talk about. No one, in fact, was at all the worse for it, except the ruffian called Bill, who, on one of Young Dave's rare visits to the Settlement, got into an argument with him on the subject, and incidentally got a licking.

Chapter XI

Miranda and Young Dave

AFTER this the cabin in the clearing ran small risk of marauders. To the most sceptical homespun philosopher in the Settlement it seemed obvious that Kirstie and Miranda had something mysterious about them, and had forsaken their kind for the fellowship of the furtive kin. No one but Old Dave had any relish for a neighbourhood where bears kept guard, and lynxes slily frequented, and caribou bulls of a haughty temper made themselves free of the barnyard. As for Young Dave, unwilling to fall foul of the folk who were so friendly to Kirstie and Miranda, he carried his traps, his woodcraft, and his cunning rifle to a tract more remote from the clearing.

Thus it came that Miranda grew to womanhood with no human companion but her mother. To her mother she stood so close that the two assimilated each other, as it were. Such education as Kirstie possessed, and such culture, narrow but significant, were Miranda's by absorption. For the rest, the quiet folk of the wood insensibly moulded her, and the great silences, and the wide wonder of the skies at night, and the solemnity of the wind. At seventeen she was a woman, mature beyond her years, but strange, with an elfish or a faun-like strangeness: as if a soul not all human dwelt in her human shape. Silent, wild, unsmiling, her sympathies were not with her own kind, but with the wild and silent folk who know not the sweetness of laughter. Yet she was given to moods of singing mirth, at long intervals; and her tenderness toward all pain, her horror of blood, were things equally alien to the wilderness creatures, her associates. It was doubtless this unbridgable divergence, combining with her sympathy and subtle comprehension, which secured her mysterious ascendency in the forest; for by this time it would never have occurred to her to step aside even for a panther or a bull moose in his fury. Something, somehow, in the air about her, told all the creatures that she was supreme.

In appearance, Miranda was a contrast to her mother, though her colouring was almost the same. Miranda was a little less than middle height, slender, graceful, fine-boned, small of hand and foot, delicate-featured, her skin toned with the clear browns of health and the open air and the matchless cosmetic of the sun. Her abundance of bronze-black hair, shot with flame-glints wheresoever the sunlight struck it, came down low over a broad, low forehead. Her eyes, in which, as we have seen, lay very much of her power over the folk of the wood, were very large and dark. They possessed a singular transparency, akin to the magical charm of the forest shadows. There was something unreal and haunting in this inexplicable clarity of her gaze, something of that mystery which dwells in the reflections of a perfect mirror of water. Her nose, straight and well modelled, was rather large than small, with nostrils alertly sensitive to discern all the wilding savours, the clean, personal scents of the clean-living creatures of the wood, and even those inexpressibly elusive perfume-heralds which, on certain days, come upon the air, forerunning the changes of the seasons. Her mouth was large, but not too large for beauty, neither thin nor full, of a vivid scarlet, mobile and mutable, yet firm, and with the edges of the lips exactly defined. Habitually reposeful and self-controlled in movement, like her mother, her repose suggested that of a bird poised upon the wing, liable at any instant to incalculable celerities; while that of Kirstie was like the calm of a hill with the eternal disrupting fire at its heart. The scarlet ribbon which Miranda the woman, like Miranda the child, wore always about her neck, seemed in her the symbol of an ineradicable strangeness of spirit, while Kirstie's scarlet kerchief expressed but the passion which burned perennial beneath its wearer's quietude.

Being in all respects natural and unselfconscious, it is not to be wondered at that Miranda was inconsistent. The truce which she had created about her — the *pax Mirandæ* — had so long kept her eyes from the hated sight of blood that she had forgotten death, and did not more than half believe in pain. Nevertheless she was still a shaft of doom to the trout in the lake and river. Fishing was a delight to her. It satisfied some fierce instinct inherited from her forefathers, which she never thought to analyze. The musical rushing of the stream; the foam and clamour of the shallow falls; the deep, black, gleaming pools with the roots of larch and hemlock overhanging; the sullen purple and amber of the eddies with their slowly swirling patches of froth, — all these allured her, though with a threat. And then the stealthy casting of the small, baited hook or glittering fly, the tense expectancy, the electrifying tug upon the line, the thrill, the exultation of the landing, and the beauty of the spotted prey, silver and vermilion, on the olive carpet of the moss! It hardly occurred to her that they were breathing, sentient creatures, these fish of the pools. She would doubtless have resented the idea of any kinship between herself and these cold inhabiters of a hostile element. In fact, Miranda was very close to nature, and she could not escape her part in nature's never ceasing war of opposites.

Late one afternoon in summer Miranda was loitering homeward from the stream with a goodly string of trout. It was a warm day and windless, and the time of year not that which favours the fisherman. But in those cold waters the fish will rise even in July and August, and Miranda's bait, or Miranda's home-tied fly, was always a killing lure to them. She carried her catch — one gaping-jawed two-pounder, and a half dozen smaller victims — strung through the crimson gills on a forked branch of alder. Her dark face was flushed; her hair (she never wore a hat) was dishevelled; her eyes were very wide and abstracted, taking in the varied shadows, — the boulders, the markings on the bark of the tree trunks, the occasional flickering moths, and the solemn little brown owl that sat in the cleft of the pine tree, yet seeming to see not these but something within or beyond them.

Suddenly, however, they were arrested by a sight which scattered their abstraction. Their focus seemed to shorten, their expression concentrated to a strained intensity, then lightened to a greyness with anger as she took a hasty step forward, and paused, uncertain for a moment what to do.

Before her was a little open glade, full of sun, secure and inviting. At its farther edge a thick-branched, low beech tree, reaching out from the confusion of trunks and vistas, cast a pleasant differentiated shade. Here in this shade a young man lay sleeping, sprawled carelessly, his head on one arm. He was tall, gaunt, clad in grey homespuns and a well-worn buckskin jacket. His red-brown hair was cut somewhat short, his light yellow moustache, long and silky, looked the lighter by contrast with the ruddy tan of his face. His rifle leaned against the tree near by, while he slept the luxurious sleep of an idle summer afternoon.

But not five paces away crouched an immense panther, flattened to the ground, watching him.

The beast was ready, at the first movement or sign of life, to spring upon the sleeper's throat. Its tail rigidly outstretched, twitched slightly at the tip. Its great, luminous eyes were so intently fixed upon the anticipated prey that it did not see Miranda's quiet approach.

To the girl the sleeper seemed something very beautiful, in the impersonal way that a splendid flower, or a tall young tree in the open, or the scarlet-and-pearl of sunrise is beautiful — not a thing as near to herself as the beasts of the wood, whom she knew. But she was filled with strange, protective fury at the thought of peril to this interesting creature. Her hesitation was but for a moment. She knew the ferocity of the panther very well, and trembled lest the sleeper should move, or twitch a muscle. She stepped up close to his side, and fixed the animal's eyes with her disconcerting gaze.

"Get off!" she ordered sharply, with a gesture of command.

The beast had doubtless a very plentiful ignorance of the English language, but gesture is a universal speech. He understood it quite clearly. He faced her eye, and endured it for some seconds, being minded to dispute its authority. Then his glance shifted, his whole attitude changed. He rose from his crouching posture, his tail drooped, his tension relaxed, he looked back over his shoulder, then turned and padded furtively away. Just as he was leaving, the man awoke with a start, sat up, gave one wondering look at Miranda, caught sight of the panther's retreating form, and reached for his rifle.

Quick as light, Miranda intervened. Stepping between his hand and its purpose, she flamed out against him with sudden anger.

"How dare you—go to shoot him!" she cried, her voice trembling.

He had sprung to his feet, and was staring at her flushed face with a mixture of admiration and bewilderment.

"But he was goin' to jump onto me!" he protested.

"Well," rejoined Miranda, curtly, "he didn't! And you've got no call to shoot him!"

"Why didn't he?" asked the young man.

"I drove him off. If I'd thought you'd shoot him, I'd have *let* him jump onto you," was the cool reply.

"Why didn't he jump onto *you?*" asked the stranger, his keen grey eyes lighting up as if he began to understand the situation.

"Because he durs'n't,—and he wouldn't want to, neither!"

"I calculate," said the stranger, holding out his hand, while a smile softened the thoughtful severity of his face, "that you must be little Mirandy."

"My name *is* Miranda," she answered, ignoring the outstretched hand; "but I'm sure I don't know who you are, coming here into my woods to kill my friends."

"I wouldn't hurt a hair of 'em!" he asserted, with a mingling of fervour and amusement. "But ain't I one o' your friends, too, Mirandy? I used to be, anyway."

He took a step nearer, still holding out a pleading hand. Miranda drew back, and put her hands behind her. "I don't know you," she persisted, but now with something of an air of wilfulness rather than of hostility. Old memories had begun to stir in forgotten chambers of her brain.

"You *used* to be friends with Young Dave," he said, in an eager half whisper. Miranda's beauty and the strangeness of it were getting into his long-untroubled blood.

The girl at once put out her hand with a frank kindness. "Oh, I remember!" she said. "You've been a long time forgetting us, haven't you? But never mind. Come along with me to the clearing, and see mother, and get some supper."

Dave flushed with pleasure at the invitation.

"Thank ye kindly, Mirandy, I reckon I will," said he; and stepping to one side he picked up his rifle. But at the sight of the weapon Miranda's new friendliness froze up, and a resentful gleam came into her great eyes.

"Let me heft it," she demanded abruptly, holding out an imperative hand.

Dave gave it up at once, with a deprecating air, though a ghost of a smile flickered under the long, yellow droop of his moustache.

Miranda had no interest in the weight or balance of the execrated weapon: possession of it was all her purpose.

"I'll carry it," she remarked abruptly. "You take these," and handing over to him the string of trout, she turned to the trail.

Dave followed, now at her side, now dropping respectfully behind, as the exigencies of the way required. Nothing was said for some time. The girl's instinctive interest in the man whom she had so opportunely protected was now quenched in antagonism, as she thought upon his murderous calling. With sharp resentment she imagined him nursing an indulgent contempt for her friendship with the furry and furtive creatures. She burned with retrospective compassion for all the beasts which had fallen to his bullets, or his blind and brutal traps. A trap was, in her eyes, the unpardonable horror. Had she not once, when a small girl, seen a lynx — perhaps it was Ganner himself — caught by the hind quarters in a dead-fall? The beast was not quite dead — it had been for days dying; its eyes were dulled, yet widely staring, and its tongue, black and swollen, stuck out between its grinning jaws. She had seen at once that the case was past relief; and she would have ended the torture had her little hands known how to kill. But helpless and anguished as she was, she had fled from the spot, and shudderingly cried her eyes out for an hour. Then it had come over her with a wrenching of remorse that the dreadful tongue craved water; and she had flown back with a tin cup of the assuaging fluid, only to find the animal just dead. The pain of thinking that she might have eased its last torments, and had not, bit the whole scene ineffaceably into her heart; and now, with this splendid trapper, the kind friend of her babyhood, walking at her side, the picture and its pangs returned with a horrible incongruity. But what most of all hardened her heart against the man was a sense of threat which his atmosphere conveyed to her,—a menace, in some vague way, to her whole system of life, her sympathies, her contentments, her calm.

Dave, on his part, felt himself deep in the cold flood of disfavour, and solicitously pondered a way of return to the sunshine of his companion's smile. His half-wild intuition told him at once that Miranda's anger was connected with his rifle, and he in part understood her aversion to his craft. He hungered to conciliate her; and as he trod noiselessly the scented gloom of the arches, the mottled greens and greys and browns of the trail, he laid his plans with far-considering prudence. It was characteristic of his quietly masterful nature that he not once thought of conciliating by giving up gun and trap and turning to a vocation more humane. No, the ways and means which occupied his thoughts were the ways and means of converting Miranda to his own point of view. He felt, though not philosophic enough to formulate it clearly, that he had all nature behind him to help mould the girl to his will, while she stood not only alone, but with a grave peril of treason in her own heart.

His silence was good policy with Miranda, who was used to silence and loved it. But being a woman, she loved another's silence even better than her own. "You are a hunter, ain't you?" she inquired at last, without turning her head.

"Yes, Mirandy."

"And a trapper, too?"

"Yes, Mirandy; so they call me."

"And you like to kill the beasts?"

"Well, yes, Mirandy, kind of, leastways, I like them; and, well, you've jest got to kill them, to live yourself. That's jest what they do, kill each other, so's they can live themselves. An' it's the only kind of life *I* can live — 'way in the woods, with the shadows, an' the silence, an' the trees, an' the sky, an' the clean smells, an' the whispers you can't never understand."

Dave shut his mouth with a firm snap at the close of this unwonted outburst. Never to any one before had he so explained his passion for the hunter's life; and now Miranda, who had turned square about, was looking at him with a curious searching expression. It disconcerted him; and he feared, under those unescapable eyes, that he had talked nonsense. Nevertheless when she spoke there was a less chilling note in her voice, though the words were not encouraging.

"If you like killing the creatures," she said slowly, "it's no place for you here. So maybe you hadn't better come to the clearing."

"I don't like killing *your* beasts, anyways," he protested eagerly. "An' ever sence I heard how you an' the bears an' the caribou was friends like, I've kep' clear the other side of the divide, an' never set a trap this side the Quah-Davic valley. As for these critters you take such stock in, Mirandy, I wouldn't harm a hair of one of 'em, I swear!"

"You hadn't better! I'd kill you myself," she rejoined sharply, with a swift, dangerous flame in her strange gaze; "or I'd set Kroof on you," she added, a gleam of mirth suddenly irradiating her face, and darkening her eyes richly, till Dave was confused by her loveliness. But he kept his wits sufficiently to perceive, as she set her face again up the trail, that he was permitted to go with her.

"Who's Kroof?" he asked humbly, stepping close to her side and ignoring the fact that the pathway, just there, was but wide enough for one.

"My best friend," answered Miranda. "You'll see at the clearing. You'd better look out for Kroof, let me tell you!"

Chapter XII

Young Dave at the Clearing

DURING the rest of the journey — a matter of an hour's walking — there was little talk between Miranda and Dave; for the ancient wood has the property that it makes talk seem trivial. With those who journey through the great vistas and clear twilight of the trees, thoughts are apt to interchange by the medium of silence and sympathy, or else to remain uncommunicated. Whatever her misgivings, her resentments and hostilities, Miranda was absorbed in her companion. So deeply was she absorbed that she failed to notice an unwonted emptiness in the shadows about her.

In very truth, the furtive folk had all fled away. The presence of the hunter filled them with instinctive fear; and in their chief defence, their moveless self-effacement, they had no more any confidence while within reach of Miranda's eyes. The stranger was like herself—and though they trusted her in all else, they knew the compulsion of nature, and feared lest she might betray them to her own kind. Therefore they held prudently aloof,—the hare and the porcupine, the fox and the red cat; the raccoon slipped into his hole in the maple tree, and the wood-mice scurried under the hemlock root, and the woodpecker kept the thickness of a tree beween his foraging and Miranda's eye. Only the careless and inquisitive partridge, sitting on a birch limb just over the trail, curiously awaited their approach; till suddenly an intuition of peril awoke him, and he fled on wild wings away through the diminishing arches. Even the little brown owl in the pine crotch snapped his bill and hissed uneasily as the two passed under his perch. Yet all these signs, that would have been to her in other moods a loud proclamation of change, now passed unnoted. Miranda was receiving a new impression, and the experience engrossed her.

Arrived at the edge of the clearing, Dave was struck by the alteration that had come over it since that day, thirteen years back, when he had aided Kirstie's flight from the Settlement. It was still bleak, and overbrooded by a vast unroutable stillness, for the swelling of the land lifted it from the forest's shelter and made it neighbour to the solitary sky. But the open fields were prosperous with blue-flowered flax, pink-and-white buckwheat, the green sombreness of potatoes, and the gallant ranks of corn; while half a dozen sleek cattle dotted the stumpy pasture. The fences were well kept. The cabin and the barn were hedged about with shining thickets of sunflower, florid holly-hocks, and scarlet-runner beans. It gave the young woodman a kind of pang,— this bit of homely sweetness projected, as it were, upon the infinite solitude of the universe. It made him think, somehow, of the smile of a lost child that does not know it is lost.

Presently, to his astonishment, there rose up from behind a blackberry coppice the very biggest bear he had ever seen. The huge animal paused at sight of a stranger, and sat up on her hind quarters to inspect him. Then she dropped again upon all fours, shuffled to Miranda's side, and affectionately smuggled her nose into the girl's palm. Dave looked on with smiling admiration. The picture appealed to him. And Miranda, scanning his face with jealous keenness, could detect therein nothing but approval.

"This is Kroof," said she, graciously.

"Never seen such a fine bear in all my life!" exclaimed the young man, sincerely enough; and with a rash unmindfulness of the reserve which governs the manners of all the furtive folk (except the squirrels), he stretched out his hand to stroke Kroof's splendid coat.

The presumption was instantly resented. With an indignant squeal Kroof swung aside and struck at the offending hand, missing it by a hair's breadth, as Dave snatched it back out of peril. A flush of anger darkened his face, but he said nothing. Miranda, however, was annoyed, feeling her hospitality dishonoured. With a harsh rebuke she slapped the bear sharply over the snout, and drew a little away from her.

Kroof was amazed. Not since the episode of the hare had Miranda struck her, and then the baby hand had conveyed no offence. Now it was different: and she felt that the tall stranger was the cause of the difference. Her heart swelled fiercely within her furry sides. She gave Miranda one look of bitter reproach, and shambled off slowly down the green alleys of the potato field.

During some moments of hesitation, Miranda looked from Kroof to Dave, and from Dave to Kroof. Then her heart smote her. With a little sob in her throat, she ran swiftly after the bear, and clung to her neck with murmured words of penitence. But Kroof, paying no attention whatever, kept her way steadily to the woods, dragging Miranda as if she had been a bramble caught on her fur.

Not till she had reached the very edge of the forest, at the sunny corner where she had been wont to play with Miranda during the far-off first years of their friendship, did the old bear stop. There she turned, sat up on her haunches, eyed the girl's face steadily for some seconds, and then licked her gently on the ear. It meant forgiveness, reconciliation; but Kroof was too deeply hurt to go back with Miranda to the cabin. In response to the girl's persuasions, she but licked her hands assiduously, as if pleading to be not misunderstood, then dropped upon all fours and moved off into the forest, leaving Miranda to gaze after her with tearful eyes.

When she went back to where the young hunter awaited her, Miranda's friendly interest had vanished, and in a chilly silence — very unlike that which had been eloquent between them a short half hour before — the two walked on up to the cabin. In Kirstie's welcome Dave found all the warmth he could wish, with never a reproach for his long years of neglect, — for which, therefore, he the more bitterly reproached himself. The best of all protections against the stings of self-reproach is the reproach of others; and of this protection Kirstie ruthlessly deprived him. She asked about all the details of his life as a solitary trapper, congratulated him on his success, appeared sympathetic toward his calling, and refrained from attempting his conversion to vegetarianism. Looking at her noble figure, her face still beautiful in its strength and calm, the young man harked back in his memory to the Settlement's scandals and decided that Frank Craig had never, of his own will, forsaken a woman so altogether gracious and desirable. He resolved that he would come often to the cabin in the clearing — even if Miranda *was* unpleasant to him.

Unpleasant she certainly was, all the evening, coldly unconscious of his presence, except, of course, at supper, where civility as well as hospitality obliged her to keep his plate supplied, and not to sour his meal with an obstinate silence.

He watched her stealthily while he talked to her mother; and the fact that her wild and subtle beauty, thrilling his blood, made ridiculous the anger in his heart, did not prevent his accomplishing a brave meal of eggs, steaming buttered pancakes with molasses, and sweet cottage cheese with currant jelly. Kirstie would not hear of his going that night, so he stayed, and slept in the bunk which his father had occupied a dozen years before.

In the morning he was diligent to help with the barnyard chores, and won golden comment from Kirstie; but he found Miranda still ice to his admiration. About breakfast time, however, Kroof reappeared, with an air of having quite forgotten the evening's little unpleasantness. Of Dave she took no notice at all, looking through, beyond, and around him; but with her return Miranda's manner became a shade less austere. Her self-reproach was mitigated when she saw that her passing interest in the newcomer had not unpardonably wronged her old friend.

Dave was bound for the Settlement, to

arrange some business of bounties and pelt sales. In spite of Kirstie's hospitable arguments, he insisted on setting out as soon as breakfast was over. As he picked up his rifle from the corner beside his bunk, Miranda, as a sign of peace between them, handed him his pouch of bullets. But not so his big powder-flask, on its gay green cord. This she took to the door, and coolly emptied its contents into a clump of burdocks. Then, with an enigmatic smile, she handed back the flask to its owner.

The young hunter was annoyed. Powder was, in his eyes, a sacred thing, and such a wanton waste of it seemed to him little less than criminal.

"That was all the powder I had 'twixt here an' the Settlement," he said, in a tone of rebuke.

"So much the better," said Miranda.

"But I don't see no sense in wastin' it that way," he persisted.

"No knowing what may happen between here and the Settlement," rejoined the girl, meaningly.

Dave flushed with anger. "Didn't I pass ye my word I'd not harm a hair of one of your beasts?" he demanded.

"Then what do you want with the powder this side of the Settlement?" she inquired, with tantalizing pertinence.

The young hunter, though steady and clear in his thought, was by no means apt in repartee, and Miranda had him at a cruel disadvantage. Confused by her last question, he blundered badly in his reply. "But — what if a painter should jump onto me, like he was goin' to yesterday?" he protested.

"I thought you promised you wouldn't harm a hair of one of them," suggested Miranda, thoughtful yet triumphant.

"Would you have me let the critter kill me, jest to keep my promise?" he asked, humour beginning to correct his vexation.

"I don't see why not," murmured Miranda. "Anyhow, you've got to do without the powder. And you needn't be frightened, Dave," — this very patronizingly, — "for your father never carries a gun on our trail, and he's never needed one yet."

"Well, then," laughed Dave, "I'll try an' keep my hair on, an' not be clean skeered to death. Good-by, Kirstie! Good-by, Mirandy! I'll look 'round this way afore long, like as not."

"Inside of twelve years?" said Kirstie, with a rare smile, which robbed her words of all reproach.

"Likely," responded Dave, and he swung off with long, active strides down the trail.

Miranda's eyes followed him with reluctance.

Chapter XIII

Milking-time

YOUNG Dave Titus was not without the rudiments of a knowledge of woman, few as had been his opportunities for acquiring that rarest and most difficult of sciences. He made no second visit to the cabin in the clearing till he had kept Miranda many weeks wondering at his absence. Then, when the stalks were whitey grey, and the pumpkins golden yellow in the corn-field, and the buck-wheat patch was crisply brown, and the scarlet of the maples was beginning to fade out along the forest edges, he came drifting back lazily one late afternoon, just as the slow *tink-a-tonk* of the cow-bells was beginning the mellow proclamation of milking-time and sundown. The tonic chill of autumn in the wilderness open caught his nostrils deliciously as he emerged from the warmer stillness of the woods. The smell, the sound of the cow-bells, — these were homely sweet after the day-long solitude of the trail. But the scene — the grey cabin lifted skyward on the gradual swell of the fields — was loneliness itself. The clearing seemed to Dave a little beautiful lost world, and it gave him an ache at the heart to think of the years that Miranda and Kirstie had dwelt in it alone.

Just beyond the edge of the forest he came upon Kroof, grubbing and munching some wild roots. He spoke to her deferentially, but she swung her huge rump about and firmly ignored him. He was anxious to win the shrewd beast's favour, or at least her tolerance, both because she had stirred his imagination and because he felt that her good-will would be, in Miranda's eyes, a most convincing testimonial to his worth. But he wisely refrained from forcing himself upon her notice.

"Go slow, my son, go slow. It's a she; an' more'n likely you don't know jest how to take her," he muttered to himself, after a fashion acquired in the interminable solitude of his camp. Leaving Kroof to her moroseness, he hastened up to the cabin, in hopes that he would be in time to help Kirstie and Miranda with the milking.

Just before he got to the door he experienced a surprise, so far as he was capable of being surprised at anything which might take place in these unreal surroundings. From behind the cabin came Wapiti the buck, or perhaps a younger Wapiti, on whom the spirit of his sire had descended in double portion. Close after him came two does, sniffing doubtfully at the smell of a stranger on the air. To Wapiti a stranger at the cabin, where such visitants were unheard of, must needs be an enemy, or at least a suspect. He stepped delicately out into the path, stamped his fine hoof in defiance, and lowered his armory of antlers. They were keen and hard, these October antlers, for this was the moon of battle, and he was ready. In rutting season Wapiti was every inch a hero.

Now Dave Titus well knew that this was no bluff of Wapiti's. He was amused and embarrassed. He could not fight this unexpected foe, for victory or defeat would be equally fatal to his hope of pleasing Miranda. As a consequence, here he was, Dave Titus, the noted hunter, the Nimrod, held up by a rutting buck! Well, the trouble was of Miranda's making. She'd have to get him out of it. Facing the defiant Wapiti at a distance of five or six paces, he rested the butt of his rifle on his toe and sent a mellow, resonant *heigh-lo, heigh-lo!* echoing over the still air. The forest edges took it up, answering again and again. Kirstie and Miranda came to the door to see who gave the summons, and they understood the situation at a glance.

"Call off yer dawg, Mirandy," cried Young Dave, "an' I'll come an' pay ye a visit."

"He thinks you're going to hurt us," explained Kirstie; and Miranda, with a gay laugh, ran to the rescue.

"You mustn't frighten the good little

boy, Wapiti," she cried, pushing the big deer out of her path and running to Dave's side. As soon as Wapiti saw Miranda with Dave, he comprehended that the stranger was not a foe. With a flourish of his horns he stepped aside and led his herd off through the barnyard.

Arriving at the door, where Kirstie, gracious, but impassive, awaited him, Dave exclaimed: "She's saved my life ag'in, Kirstie, that girl o' yourn. First it's a painter, an' now it's a rutting buck. Wonder what it'll be next time!"

"A rabbit, like as not, or a squir'l, maybe," suggested Miranda, unkindly.

"Whatever it be," persisted Dave, "third time's luck for me, anyways. If you save my life agin, Mirandy, you'll hev' to take care o' me altogether. I'll git to kind of depend on ye."

"Then I reckon, Dave, you'll get out of your next scrape by yourself," answered Miranda, with discouraging decision.

"That's one on you, Dave," remarked Kirstie, with a strictly neutral air. But behind Miranda's back she shot him a look which said, "Don't you mind what she says, she's all right in her heart!" which, indeed, was far from being the case. Had Dave been so injudicious as to woo openly at this stage of Miranda's feelings, he would have been dismissed with speedy emphasis.

Dave was in time to help with the milking, — a process which he boyishly enjoyed. The cows, five of them, were by now lowing at the bars. Kirstie brought out three tin pails. "You can help us, if you like, Dave," she cried, while Miranda looked her doubt of such a clumsy creature's capacity for the gentle art of milking. "Can you milk?" she asked.

"'Course I can, though I haven't had much chance, o' late years, to practise," said Dave.

"Can you milk without hurting the cow? Are you sure? And can you draw off the strippings clean?" she persisted, manifestly sceptical.

"Try me," said Dave.

"Let him take old Whitey, Miranda.

He'll get through with her, maybe, while we're milking the others," suggested Kirstie.

"Oh, well, any one could milk Whitey," assented Miranda; and Dave, on his mettle, vowed within himself that he'd have old Whitey milked, and milked dry, and milked to her satisfaction, before either Kirstie or Miranda was through with her first milker. He stroked the cow on the flank, and scratched her belly gently, and established friendly relations with her before starting; and the elastic firmness of his strong hands chanced to suit Whitey's large teats. The animal eyed him with favour and gave down her milk affluently. As the full streams sounded more and more liquidly in his pail, Dave knew that he had the game in his hands, and took time to glance at his rivals. To his astonishment there was Kroof standing up on her haunches close beside Miranda, her narrow red tongue lolling from her lazily open jaws, while she watched the milky fountains with interest.

While Kirstie's scarlet kerchiefed head

was still pressed upon her milker's flank, and while Miranda was just beginning to draw off the rich "strippings" into a tin cup, Dave completed his task. His pail — he had milked the strippings in along with the rest — was foaming creamily to the brim. He arose and vaunted himself. "Some day, when I've got lots of time," he drawled, "I'll l'arn you two how to milk."

"You needn't think you're done already," retorted Miranda, without looking up. "I'll get a quart more out of old Whitey, soon as I'm through here."

But Kirstie came over and looked at the pail. "No, you won't, Miranda, not this time," she exclaimed. "Dave's beaten us, sure. Old Whitey never gave us a fuller pail in her life. Dave, you *can* milk. You go and milk Michael over there, the black-an'-white one, for me. I'll leave you and Miranda, if you won't fall out, to finish up here, while I go and get an extra good supper for you, so's you'll come again soon. I know you men keep your hearts in your stomachs, just where we women know how to reach them easy. Where'd we have been if the Lord hadn't made us cooks!"

Such unwonted pleasantry on the part of her sombre mother proved to Miranda that Dave was much in her graces, and she felt moved to a greater austerity in order that she might keep the balance true. Throughout the rest of the milking, she answered all Dave's attempts at conversation with briefest *yes* or *no*, and presently reduced him to a discouraged silence. During supper, — which consisted of fresh trout fried in corn meal, and golden hot johnny-cake with red molasses, and eggs fried with tomatoes, and sweet curds with clotted cream, all in a perfection to justify Kirstie's promise, — Miranda relented a little, and talked freely. But Dave had been too much subdued to readily regain his cheer. It was his tongue now that knew but *yes* and *no*. Confronted by this result of her unkindness, Miranda's sympathetic heart softened. Turning in her seat to slip a piece of johnny-cake, drenched in molasses, into the expectant mouth of Kroof who sat up beside her, she spoke to Dave in a tone whose sweetness thrilled him to the finger-tips. The instinct of coquetry, native and not unknown to the furtive folk themselves, was beginning to stir within Miranda's untaught heart.

"I'm going down to the lake to-night, Dave," she said, "to set a night line and see if I can catch a togue.[1] There's a full moon, and the lake'll be worth looking at. Won't you come along with us?"

"Won't I, Miranda? Couldn't think of nothin' I'd like better!" was the eager response.

"We'll start soon as ever we get the dishes washed up," explained the girl. "And you can help us at that — what say, mother?"

"Certainly, Dave can help us," answered Kirstie, "if you have the nerve to set the likes of him at woman's work. But I reckon I won't go with you to-night to the lake. Kroof and Dave'll be enough to look after you."

[1] A species of large, grey lake trout.

"I'll look after Dave, more like," exclaimed Miranda, scornfully, remembering both Wapiti and the panther. "But what's the matter, mother? *Do* come. It won't be the same without you."

"Seems to me I'm tired to-night, kind of, and I just want to stay at home by the fire and think."

Miranda sprang up, with concern in her face, and ran round to her mother's seat.

"Tired, mother!" she cried, scanning her features anxiously. "Who ever heard of people like you and me, who are strong, and live right, being tired? I'm afraid you're not well, mother; I won't go one step!"

"Yes, you will, dearie," answered her mother, and never yet had Miranda rebelled against that firm note in Kirstie's voice. "I really want to be alone to-night a bit, and think. Dave's visit has stirred up a lot of old thoughts, and I want to take a look at them. I reckoned they were dead and buried years ago!"

"Are you sure you're not sick, mother?"

went on Miranda, hesitatingly returning to her seat.

"No, child, I'm not sick. But I have felt tired off an' on the last few days when there was no call to. I do begin to feel that this big solitude of the woods is wearing on me, someway. I've stood up under it all these years, Dave, and it's given me peace and strength when I needed it bad enough, God knows. But someway I reckon it's too big for me, and will crush me in the long run. I love the clearing, but I don't just want to end my days here."

"Mother," cried Miranda, springing up again, "I never heard you talk so before in my life! Leave the clearing! Leave the woods! I *couldn't* live, I just couldn't, anywheres else at all!"

"There's other places, Miranda," murmured Dave. But Kirstie continued the argument.

"It's a sight different with you, child," she said thoughtfully. "You've grown up here. The woods and the sky have made you. They're in your blood. You live and breathe them. You were a queer baby — more a fairy or a wild thing than a human youngster — before ever you came to the clearing; and all the wild things seem to think you're one of themselves; and you see what other folks can't see — what the folks of the woods themselves can't see. Oh, yes! it's a sight different with you, Miranda. Your father used to watch you and say you'd grow up to be a faun woman or wood goddess, or else the fairies would carry you off. This place is all right for you. And I used to think I was that big and strong of spirit that I could stand up to it all the rest of my life. But I begin to think it's too big for me. I don't want to die here, Miranda!"

Miranda stared at her, greatly troubled. "You won't die till I'm old enough to die too, mother," she cried, "for I just couldn't live without you one day. But," she added passionately, "I know I should die, quick, right off, if I had to go away from the clearing! I know I would!"

She spoke with the fiercer positiveness, because, just as she was speaking, there came over her a doubt of her own words. In a flash she saw herself growing old here in the vast solitude, she and Kirstie together, and no one else anywhere to be seen. The figure so cruelly conspicuous in its absence bore a strange, dim likeness to Young Dave. She did not ask herself if it were possible that she could one day wish to desert the clearing, and the stillnesses, and all the folk of the ancient wood, but somewhere at the back of her heart she felt that it might even be so, and her heart contracted poignantly. She ran and flung both arms about Kroof's neck, and wiped a stealthy tear on the shaggy coat.

Dave, with a quickening intuition born of his dread lest the trip to the lake should fall through, saw that the conversation was treading dangerous ground. He discreetly changed the subject to johnny-cake.

Chapter XIV

Moonlight and Moose-call

WHEN Miranda was ready to start, the moon was up, low and large, shining broadly into the cabin window. Miranda brought forward a small, tin-covered kettle, containing some little fish for bait.

"Where's your line an' hooks?" asked Dave.

"I keep them in a hollow tree by the lake," said Miranda. "But don't you go to take that thing along, or you don't go with me!" she added sharply, as the young man picked up his rifle.

He set it down again with alacrity.

"But at night, Mirandy!" he protested. "Air ye sure it's safe?"

"Don't come if you're afraid!" she answered witheringly, stepping out into the white light and the coldly pungent air.

Dave was at her side in a moment, ignoring a taunt which could touch him least among men. At Miranda's other side was the great lumbering form of Kroof, with the girl's hand resting lovingly on her neck.

"We'll not be long, mother," called Miranda to Kirstie, in the doorway.

But before they had gone twenty paces, Kroof stopped short, and sat down to deliberate. She regarded it as her own peculiar office to protect Miranda (who needed no protection) on these nocturnal expeditions to which the girl was given in some moods. Was the obnoxious stranger to usurp her office and her privilege? Well, she would not share with him. She would stay where she was needed.

"Come along, Kroof!" urged Miranda, with a little tug at her fur. But the jealous bear was obstinate. She wheeled and made for the cabin door.

Miranda was irritated.

"Let her stay, then!" she exclaimed, setting her face to the forest, and smiling in more gracious fashion upon Young Dave. Kroof was certainly very provoking.

"That's all right!" said Dave, more pleased than he dare show. "She'll be company for yer mother till we git back."

"Kroof seems to think she owns me!" mused Miranda. "I love her better than any one else in the world except mother; but I mustn't spoil her when she gets cross about nothing. She oughtn't to be so jealous when I'm nice to you, Dave! I'm very angry at her for being so silly. She ought to know you're nothing to me alongside of her; now, oughtn't she?"

"Of course," assented Dave, with such cheerfulness as he could assume. Then he set himself craftily to win Miranda's approval by a minute account of the characteristics — mental, moral, and physical — of a tame bear named Pete, belonging to one of the lumbermen at the Settlement. The subject was sagaciously chosen, and had the effect of making Miranda feel measurably less remote from the world of men. It suggested to her a kind of possible understanding between the world of men and the world of the ancient wood.

As they left the moonlit open, the long white fingers of the phantom light reached after them, down the dissolving arches. Then the last groping ray was left behind, and they walked in the soft dark. Dave found it an exquisite but imperative necessity to keep close at Miranda's elbow, touching her very skirt indeed, for even his trained woodland eyes could at first distinguish nothing. Miranda, however, with her miraculous vision, moved swiftly, unhesitatingly, as if in broad day and a plain way.

Soon, however, Dave's eyes adapted themselves, and he could discern vague differences, denser masses, semi-translucencies in the enfolding depth of blackness. For there *was* a light, of a kind, carried down by countless reflections and refractions from the lit, wet surfaces of the topmost leaves. Moreover, clean-blooded and fine-nerved as he was from his years of living under nature's ceaseless purgation, his other senses came to the aid of his baffled sight. He seemed to feel, rather than see, the massive bulk of the pine and birch trunks as his face approached them to the nearness of an arm's length. He felt, too, an added hardness and a swelling under the moss, wherever the network of roots came close to the parent trunk. His nostrils discerned the pine, the spruce, the hemlock, the balsam poplar, the aromatic moosewood, as he passed them; and long before he came to it he knew the tamarack swamp was near. Only his ears could not aid him. Except for Miranda's footsteps, feather-soft upon the moss, and his own heavier but skilfully muffled tread, there was no sound in the forest but an indeterminate whisper, so thin that it might have been the speech of the leaves conferring, or the sap climbing through the smaller branches. Neither he nor Miranda uttered a word. The stillness was such that a voice would have profaned it. Finding it difficult to keep up without stumbling and making a rough noise, Dave frankly resigned himself to the girl's superior craft.

"You've got to be eyes fer me here, you wonderful Mirandy, er I can't keep up with ye!" he whispered at her ear. The light warmth of his breath upon her neck made her tingle in a way that bewildered her; but she found it pleasant. When he took hold of her arm, very gently, to steady himself, rather to his surprise he was permitted. He was wise enough, however, not to attach too much importance to the favour. He pondered the fact that to Miranda, who was not a Settlement girl, it meant altogether nothing.

Presently, just ahead of them, they saw a pair of palely-glowing eyes, about two feet from the ground. Miranda squeezed the hand inside her arm, as a sign that Dave was not to regret his rifle. As a matter of fact, he was not disposed to regret anything at that moment.

"*Lou'-cerfie!*" he whispered at her ear, meaning the lynx, or *loup-cervier* of the camps.

"No, panther!" murmured Miranda, indifferently, going straight forward. At this startling word, Dave could not, under the circumstances, refrain from a certain misgiving. A panther is not good to meet in the dark. But the palely-glowing eyes sank mysteriously toward the ground and retreated as Miranda advanced; and in a few seconds they went floating off to one side and disappeared.

"How on earth do ye do it, Mirandy?" whispered Dave, rather awestruck.

"They know me," replied the girl; which seemed to her, but not to Dave, an all-sufficient answer.

There was no more said. The magic of the dark held them both breathless. They were strung to a strange, electric pitch of sympathy and expectation. Dave's fingers, where they rested on the girl's arm, tingled curiously, deliciously. Once, close beside them, there was a sharp rattle of claws going up the bark of a fir tree, and then two little points of light, close together, gleamed down upon them from overhead. Both Miranda and Dave knew it was a raccoon, and said nothing. Farther on they came suddenly upon a spectrally luminous figure just in their path. It was nearly the height of a man. The ghostly light waxed and waned before their eyes. A timorous imagination might have been pardoned for calling it a spirit sent to warn them back from their venture. But they knew it was only a rotting birch stump turned phosphorescent. As they passed, Dave broke off a piece and crumbled it, and for some minutes the bluish light clung to his fingers, like a perfume.

At last they heard an owl hoot solemnly in the distance. "*Tw'oh-hoo-hoo-hoo-ooo*," it went, a cold and melancholy sound.

"We're near the lake," whispered Miranda. "I know Wah-hoo; he lives in an old tree close to the water. We're almost there." Then glimpses of light came, broken and thin, from the far-off moon-silvered surface. Then a breath of chill, though there was no wind. And then they came out upon the open shore.

Miranda, with a decisive gesture, removed her arm from Dave's grasp, and side by side the two followed the long sweep of sandy beach curving off to the right.

"See that point yonder," said Miranda, "with the lop-sided tree standing alone on it? I've got my line and hooks hidden in that tree."

"How do ye set a night line without a boat?" queried Dave.

"Got one, of course!" answered the girl. "Your father made me a dugout, last summer a year ago, and I keep it drawn up behind the point."

The moon was high now, sailing in icy splendour of solitude over the immensity of the ancient wood. The lake was a windless mirror. The beach was very smooth and white, etched along its landward edges with the shadows of the trees. At one spot a cluster of three willows grew very near the water's brink, spreading a transparent and mysterious shadow. Just as Dave and Miranda came to this little oasis in the shining sand, across the water came the long, sonorous call of a bull moose. It was a deep note, melodious and far carrying, and seemed in some way the very spoken thought of the vastness.

"That's what I call music!" said Dave.

But before Miranda could respond, a thunderous bellow roared in answer from the blackness of the woods close by; there was a heavy crashing in the underbrush, and the towering front of another bull appeared at the edge of the sands, looking for his challenger. Catching sight of Dave and Miranda, he charged down upon them at once.

"Get up a tree, quick!" cried Dave, slipping his long knife from its sheath and stepping in front of the girl.

"Don't you meddle and there'll be no trouble!" said Miranda, sharply. "You stand behind that tree!" and seizing him by the arm she attempted to push him out of sight. But for a second he stupidly resisted.

"Fool!" she flamed out at him. "What do you suppose I've done all these years without you?"

The anger in her eyes pierced his senses and brought wisdom. He realized that somehow she was master of the situation, and he reluctantly stepped behind the big willow trunk. It was just in the nick of time, for the furious animal was almost upon them. At this moment a breath of air from the water carried Miránda's scent to the beast's nostrils, and he checked himself in doubt. At once Miranda gave a soft whistle and stepped out into the clear flood of moonlight. The moose recognized her, stood still, raised his gigantic antlers to their full height, and stretched toward her his long, flexible snout, sniffing amicably. Then, step by step, he approached, while she waited with her small hand held out to him, palm upward; and Dave looked on in wonder from behind his tree, still doubtful, his fingers gripping his knife-hilt.

At this moment the first call sounded again across the lake. The moose forgot Miranda. He wheeled nimbly, lowered his head toward the great challenge, bellowed his answer, and charged along the shore to mortal combat. As he disappeared around a jutting spur of pines, a tall cow moose emerged from the shades and trotted after him.

Miranda turned to Dave with an air of triumph, her anger forgotten.

"I swan, Mirandy!" exclaimed the young hunter, "the girl as can manage a bull moose in callin' season is the Queen of the Forest, sure. I take off my cap to yer majesty!"

"Put it on again, Dave," said she, not half displeased, "and we'll go set the night lines."

Behind the point, hidden in a thicket of mixed huckleberry and ironwood, they found the wooden canoe, or dugout, in good condition. Dave ran it down into the water, and Miranda tossed in a roll of stout cod-line, with four large hooks depending from it, at four-foot intervals, by drop strings a foot and a half in length. The hooks she proceeded to bait from the tin kettle.

"Why don't ye have more hooks on sech a len'th of line?" inquired Dave.

"Don't want to catch more togue than we can eat," explained Miranda. "It's no fun catching them this way, and they're not much good salted."

There was but one paddle, and this Dave captured. "You sit in the bow, Mirandy, an' see to the lines, an' I'll paddle ye out," said he.

But Miranda would have none of it. "Look here, Dave," she exclaimed, "I'm doing this, and you're just a visitor. I declare, I'm almost sorry I brought you along. You just sit where you're put, and do as I tell you, or you won't come with me again."

The young man squatted himself meekly on his knees, a little forward of amidship, but not far enough for his superior weight to put the canoe down by the bow. Then Miranda stepped in delicately, seated herself on a thwart at the stern, and dipped her paddle with precise and masterful stroke. The canoe shot noiselessly out of the shadow and into the unrippled sheen. Just off the point, about twenty yards from shore, lay a light wooden float at anchor. Beside this Miranda brought her canoe to a standstill, backing water silently with firm flexures of her wrist. To a rusty staple in the float she fastened one end of the line.

"Deep water off this here point, I reckon," commented Dave.

"Of course," answered Miranda. "The togue only lie in deep water."

Dave was permitted to make comments, but to take no more active part in the proceedings. As he was a man of deeds and dreams rather than of speech, this was not the rôle he coveted, and he held his tongue; while Miranda, deftly paying out the line with one hand, with the other cleverly wielded the paddle so that the canoe slipped toward shore. She was too much absorbed in the operation to vouchsafe any explanation to Dave, but he saw that she intended making fast the other end of the line to a stake which jutted up close to the water's edge.

Miranda now slipped the line under her foot to hold it, and, taking both hands to her paddle, was about to make a landing, when suddenly there was a violent tug at one of the hooks. The line was torn from under her light foot, and at once dragged overboard. Dave saw what had happened; but he was wise enough not to say, even by look or tone, "I told you so!" Instead, he turned and pointed to the float, which was now acting very erratically, darting from side to side, and at times plunging quite under water. The glassy mirror of the lake was shattered to bits.

"You've got him a'ready, Mirandy," he cried in triumph; and his palpable elation quite covered Miranda's chagrin. Two or three strong strokes of her paddle brought the canoe back to the float, and Dave had his reward.

"Catch hold of the float, Dave," she commanded, "and pull him aboard, while I hold the canoe."

With a great splashing and turmoil he hauled up a large togue, of twelve pounds or thereabouts, and landed it flopping in the bottom of the dugout. A stroke in the back of the neck from Miranda's knife.

sharp but humane, put a term to its struggles.

While Dave gazed admiringly at the glittering spoil, Miranda began untying the line from the float.

"What air ye doin' now, Mirandy?" he inquired, as she proceeded to strip the bait from the remaining hooks, and throw the pieces overboard.

"We won't want any more togue for a week," she explained. "This is such a fine, big one." And she headed the canoe for the landing-place, under the shadow of the point.

Chapter XV

A Venison Steak

THROUGHOUT the succeeding winter Dave managed to visit the clearing two or three times in the course of each month, but he could not see that he made any progress in Miranda's favour. As at first, she was sometimes friendly, sometimes caustically indifferent. Only once did he perceive in her the smallest hint of gratification at his coming. That was the time when he came on his snowshoes through the forest by moonlight, the snow giving a diffused glimmer that showed him the trail even through the densest thickets. Arriving in the morning, he surprised her at the door of the cow stable, where she had been foddering the cattle. Her face flushed at the sight of him; and a look came into her wide, dark eyes which even his modesty could not quite misunderstand. But his delight quickly crumbled. Miranda was loftily indifferent to him during all that visit, so much so that after he had gone Kirstie reproached her with incivility.

"I can't help it, mother!" she explained. "I don't want to hate him, but what better is he than a butcher? His bread is stained with blood. Pah! I sometimes think I smell blood, the blood of the kind wood creatures, when he's around."

"But you don't want him not to come, girl, surely," protested her mother.

"Well, you know, it's a pleasure to you to have him come once in a while," said the girl, enigmatically.

Dave continued his visits, biding his time. He lost no chance of familiarizing Miranda's imagination with the needs of man as he imagined them, and with a rational conception of life as he conceived it. This he did not directly, but through the medium of conversation with Kirstie, to whom his words were sweetness. He was determined to break down Miranda's prejudice against his calling, which to him was the only one worth a man's while,—wholesome, sane, full of adventure, full of romance. He was determined, also, to overcome her deep aversion to flesh food. He felt that not till these two points were gained would Miranda become sufficiently human to understand human love or any truly human emotions. In this belief he strictly withheld his wooing, and waited till the barriers that opposed it should be undermined by his systematic attacks. He was too little learned in woman to realize that with Miranda his best wooing was the absence of all wooing; and so he builded better than he knew.

During the cold months he was glad to be relieved of the presence of Kroof, who had proved, in her taciturn way, quite irreconcilable. He had tried in vain to purchase her favour with honey, good hive bees' honey in the comb, carried all the way from the Settlement. She would have nothing to do with him at any price; and he felt that this discredited him in Miranda's eyes. He hoped that Kroof would sleep late that spring in her lair under the pine root.

But while Dave was labouring so assiduously, and, as he fancied, so subtly, to mould and fashion Miranda, she all unawares was moulding him. Unconsciously his rifle and his traps were losing zest for him; and the utter solitude of his camp beyond the Quah-Davic began to have manifest disadvantages. Once he hesitated so long over a good shot at a lynx, just because the creature looked unsuspecting, that in the end he was too late, and his store of pelts was the poorer by one good skin. Shooting a young cow moose in the deep snow, moreover, he felt an unwonted qualm when the gasping and bleeding beast turned upon him a look of anguished reproach. His hand was not quite so steady as usual when he gave her the knife in the throat. This was a weakness which he did not let himself examine too closely. He knew the flesh of the young cow was tender and good, and after freezing it he hung it up in his cold cellar. Though he would not for an instant have acknowledged it, even to himself, he was glad that bears were not his business during the winter, for he would almost certainly have felt a sense of guilt, of wrong to Miranda, in shooting them. For all this undercurrent of qualm in the hidden depths of his heart, however, his hunting was never more prosperous than during the January and February of that winter; and fox, lynx, wolverine, seemed not only to run upon his gun, but to seek his traps as a haven. He killed with an emphasis, as if to rebuke the waking germ of softness in his soul. But he had little of the old satisfaction, as he saw his peltries accumulate. His craft was now become a business, a mere routine necessity. For pleasure, he chose to watch Miranda as her feathered pensioners — snowbirds, wrens, rose grosbeaks, and a glossy crow or two — gathered about her of a morning for their meal of grain and crumbs. They alighted on her hair, her shoulders, her arms; and the round-headed, childlike grosbeaks would peck bread from her red lips; and a crow, every now and then, would sidle in briskly and give a mischievous tug at the string of her moccasin. To the girl, his heart needed no warming, — it burned by now with a fire which all his backwood's stoicism could but ill disguise, — but to the birds, and through them to all the furry folk of the wood, his heart warmed as he regarded the beautiful sight. He noted that the birds were quite unafraid of Kirstie, who also fed them; but he saw that toward Miranda they showed an active, even aggressive ardour, striving jealously for the touch of her hand or foot or skirt when no tit-bits whatever were in question. And another sight there was, toward shut of winter's evening, that moved him strangely. The wild, white hares (he and Kirstie and Miranda called them rabbits) would come leaping over the snow to the cabin door to be fed, with never cat or weasel on their trail. They would press around the girl, nibbling eagerly at her dole of clover, hay, and carrots; some crouching about her feet, some erect and striking at her petticoat with their nervous fore paws, all twinkling-eared, and all implicitly trustful of this kind Miranda of the clover.

Toward spring Miranda began to be troubled about Kirstie's health. She saw that the firm lines of her mother's face were growing unwontedly sharp, the bones of her cheek and jaw strangely conspicuous. Then her solicitous scrutiny took note of a pallor under the skin, a greyish whiteness at the corners of her eyes, a lack of vividness in the usually brilliant scarlet of the lips; for up to now Kirstie had retained all the vital colouring and tone of youth. Then, too, there was a listlessness, a desire to rest and take breath after very ordinary tasks of chopping or of throwing fodder for the cattle. This puzzled the girl much more than Kirstie's increasing tendency to sit dreaming over the hearth fire when there was work to be done. Miranda felt equal to doing all the winter work, and she knew that her mother, like herself, was ever a dreamer when the mood was on. But even this brooding abstraction came to worry her at last, when one morning, after a drifting storm which had piled the snow halfway up the windows, her mother let her shovel out all the paths unaided, with never a comment or excuse. Miranda was not aggrieved at this, by any means; but she began to be afraid, sorely afraid. It was so unlike the alert and busy Kirstie of old days. Of necessity, Miranda turned to Dave for counsel in her alarm, when next he came to the clearing.

The conference took place in the warm twilight of the cow stable, where Dave, according to his custom, was helping Miranda at the milking, while Kirstie got supper. The young hunter looked serious, but not surprised.

"I've took note o' the change this two month back, Mirandy," he said, "an' was a-wonderin' some how them big eyes of yourn, that can see things us ordinary folks can't see, could be blind to what teched ye so close."

"I *wasn't* blind to it, Dave," protested the girl, indignantly; "but I didn't see how you could help any. Nor I don't see now; but there was no one else I could speak to about it," she added, with a break in her voice that distantly presaged tears.

"I could help some, if you'd let me, Mirandy," he hesitated, "for I know right well what she's needin'."

"Well, what is it?" demanded the girl. There was that in his voice which oppressed her with a vague misgiving.

"It's good, fresh, roast meat she wants!" said Dave.

There was a pause. Miranda turned and looked out through the stable door, across the glimmering fields.

"It's her blood's got thin an' poor," continued Dave. "Nothin' but flesh meat'll build her up now, an' she's jest got to have it." He was beginning to feel it was time that Miranda experienced the touch of a firm hand.

"I don't believe you!" said the girl, and turned hotly to her milking.

"Well, we'll see," retorted Dave. In Miranda's silence he read a tardy triumph for his views.

That evening he took note of the fact that Kirstie came to supper with no appetite, though every dish of it was tempting and well cooked. Miranda observed this also. Her fresh pang of apprehension on her mother's account was mixed with a resentful feeling that Dave would interpret every symptom as a confirmation of his own view. She was quite honest in her rejection of that view, for in her eyes flesh food was a kind of subtle poison. But she was too anxious about her mother's health to commit herself in open hostility to anything, however extreme, which might be suggested in remedy. On this point she was resolved to hold aloof, letting the decision rest between her mother and Dave.

Aroused by the young hunter's talk, Kirstie was brighter than usual during the meal; but, to her great disappointment, Dave got up to go immediately after supper. He would take no persuasion, but insisted that he had come just to see if she and Miranda were well, and declared that affairs of supreme importance called him straight back to the camp. Kirstie was not convinced. She turned a face of reproach on Miranda, so frankly that the girl was compelled to take her meaning.

"Oh! it isn't my fault, mother," she protested, with a little vexed laugh. "I've not been doing anything ugly to him. If he goes, it's just his own obstinacy, for he knows we'd like him to stay as he always does. Let him go if he wants to!"

"Mirandy," said her mother, in a voice of grave rebuke, "I wish you would not be so hard with Dave. If you treated your dumb beasts like you treat him, I reckon they would never come to you a second time. You seem to forget that Dave and his father are our only friends, —and just now, Dave's father being in the lumber camp, we've nobody but Dave here to look to."

"Oh! I've nothing against Dave, mother, except the blood on his hands," retorted the girl, turning her face away.

The young hunter shrugged his shoulders, deprecatingly, smiled a slow smile of understanding at Kirstie, and strode to the door.

"Good night, both of ye," he said cheerfully. "Ye'll see me back, liker'n not, by this time to-morrow."

As he went, Miranda noticed with astonishment and a flush of warmth that for once in his career he was without his inseparable rifle. Kirstie, in the vacant silence that followed his going, had it on her tongue to say, "I do wish you could take to Dave, Miranda." But the woman's heart within her gave her warning in time, and she held her peace. Thanks to this prudence, Miranda went to bed that night with something of a glow at her heart. Dave's coming without the rifle was a direct tribute to her influence, and to some extent outweighed his horrible suggestion that her mother should defile her mouth with meat.

The next evening the chores were all done up; the "rabbits" had come and gone with their clover and carrots; and Kirstie and Miranda were sitting down to their supper, when in walked Dave. He carried a package of something done up in brown sacking. This time, too, he carried his rifle. Kirstie's welcome was frankly eager, but Miranda saw the rifle, and froze. He caught her look, and with a flash of intuition understood it.

"*Had* to bring it along, Mirandy," he explained, with a flush of embarrassment. "Couldn't ha' got here without it. The wolves have come back again, six of 'em. They set on to me at my own camp door."

"Oh, wolves!" exclaimed Miranda, in a tone of aversion. "They're vermin."

Since that far-off day when, with her childish face flattened against the pane, her childish heart swelling with wrath and tears, she had watched the wolves attack Ten-Tine's little herd, she had hated the ravening beasts with a whole-souled hate.

"I hope to goodness you killed them all!" said Kirstie, with pious fervour.

"Two got off; got the pelts of the others," answered Dave.

"Not too bad, that," commented

Kirstie, with approval; "now come and have some supper."

"Not jest yet, Kirstie," he replied, undoing his package. "I've noticed lately ye was looking mighty peaked, an' hadn't much appetite, like. Now when folks has anything the matter with 'em I know as much about it as lots of the doctors, and I know what's goin' to set ye right up. If ye'll lend me the loan of yer fire, an' a frying-pan, I'll have something for yer supper that'll do ye more good than a bucketful of doctor's medicine."

Miranda knew what was coming. She knew Dave had been all the way back to the camp, beyond the Quah-Davic, for meat, that he might run no risk of killing any of the beasts that were under her protection. She knew, too, that to make such a journey in the twenty-four hours he could scarce have had one hour's sleep. None the less, she hardened her heart against him. She kept her eyes on her plate and listened with strained intensity for her mother's word upon this vital subject.

Kirstie's interest was now very much awake. "There's the fire, Dave," she said, "and there's the frying-pan hanging on the side of the dresser. But what have you got? I've felt this long while I'd like a bit of a change — not but what the food we're used to, Miranda and me, is real good food and wholesome."

"Well, Kirstie," he answered, taking a deep breath before the plunge, and at the same time throwing back the wrapping from a rosy cut of venison steak, "it's jest nothin' more nor less than fresh meat. It's venison, clean an' wholesome; and I'll fry ye right now this tender slice I'm cuttin' for ye."

Kirstie was startled quite out of her self-possession. The rule of the cabin against flesh meat was so long established, so well known at the Settlement, so fenced about with every sanction of principle and prejudice, that Dave's words were of the nature of a challenge. She felt that she ought to be angry; but, as a matter of fact, she was only uneasy as to how Miranda would take so daring a proposal.

At the same time she was suddenly conscious of an unholy craving for the forbidden thing. She glanced anxiously at Miranda, but the girl appeared to be wrapped up in her own thoughts.

"But you know, Dave," she protested rebukingly, "we neither of us ever touch meat of any kind. You know our opinions on this point."

The words themselves would have satisfied Miranda had she not detected a certain irresolution in the tone. They did not affect Dave in the least. For a moment he made no reply, for he was busy cutting thin slices off the steak. He spread them carefully in the hot butter, now spluttering in the pan over the coals; and then, straightening himself up from the task, knife in hand, he answered cheerfully: "That's all right. But, ye see, Kirstie, all the folks reckon me somethin' of a doctor, an' this here meat I'm cookin' for ye ain't rightly food at all. It's medicine; 't ain't right ye should hold off now, when ye need it as medicine. 'T ain't fair to Mirandy. I can see ye've jest been pinin' away like, all winter. It's new blood, with iron in it, ye need. It's flesh meat, an' flesh meat only, that'll give ye iron an' new blood. When ye're well, an' yer old strong self agin, ye can quit meat if ye like, — an' kick me out o' the cabin for interferin'; but now —"

He paused dramatically. He had talked right on, contrary to his silent habit, for a purpose. He knew the power of natural cravings. He was waiting for Kirstie's elemental bodily needs to speak out in support of his argument. He waited just time for the savoury smell of the steak to fill the cabin and work its miracle. Now the spell was abroad. He looked to Kirstie for an answer.

The instant she smelled that savour Kirstie knew that he was right. Steak, venison steak fried in butter, *was* what she required. For weeks she had had no appetite; now she was ravenous. Moreover, a thousand lesser forces, set in motion by Dave's long talks, were impelling her to just such a change as the eating of flesh would symbolize to her. But —

Miranda? Kirstie stared at her in nervous apprehension, expecting an outburst of scorn. But Miranda was seemingly oblivious of all that went on in the cabin. Her unfathomed eyes, abstractedly wide open, were staring out through the white square of the window. She was trying hard to think about the mysterious blue-white wash of radiance that seemed to pour in palpable floods from the full moon; — about the furred and furtive creatures passing and repassing noiselessly, as she knew, across the lit patches of the glades; — about the herd of moose down in the firwoods, sleeping securely between walls of deep snow in the "yard," which they had trodden for themselves a fortnight back; — of Kroof, coiled in her warm den under the pine root, with five feet of drift piled over her. But in reality she was steeling herself, with fierce desperation, against a strange appetite which was rising within her at the call of that insidious fragrance. With a kind of horror she realized that she was at war with herself — that one half her nature was really more than ready to partake of the forbidden food.

Dave noticed the look of question which Kirstie had turned upon Miranda.

"Oh, ye needn't look to her, Kirstie, to back ye up in no foolishness," he went on. "I spoke to her last night about it, an' she hadn't a word to say agin my medicine."

Still there was no comment from Miranda. If Miranda, to whom abstinence from flesh was a religion, could tolerate a compromise, why she herself, to whom it was merely a prejudice and a preference, might well break an ancient rule for an instant's good. She had been inwardly anxious for months about her condition. After a second or two of doubt, her mind was made up; and when Kirstie made up her mind, it was in no halfway fashion.

"I'll try your doctoring, Dave," she said slowly. "I'll give it a fair trial. But while you're about it, why don't you cook enough for yourself, too? Have you put salt in the pan? And here's a dash of pepper."

"No," answered the young hunter,

concealing his elation as he sprinkled the steak temperately with the proffered salt and pepper, "I don't want none myself, I need meat onct in a while, er I git weak an' no good. But there's nothin' suits my taste like the feeds I git here, — the pipin' hot riz buckwheat cakes, with lots o' butter an' molasses, an' the johnny-cake, an' the potater pie, an' the tasty ways ye cook eggs. I often think when I'm here that I wouldn't care if I never seen a slice o' fresh meat, er even bacon, agin. But our bodies is built a certain way, an' there's no gittin' over Nature's intention. We've got the teeth to prove it, an' the insides, too, — I've read all about it in doctors' books. I read a heap in camp. Fact is, Kirstie, we're built like the bear, — to live on all kinds of food, includin' flesh, — an' if we don't git all kinds onct in a while, somethin's bound to go wrong."

Never had Dave talked so much before; but now he was feverishly eager to have no opening for discussion. While he talked the venison was cooked and served. Kirstie ate it with a relish, which convinced him of the wisdom of his course. She ate all that he had fried; and he wisely refrained from cooking more, that her appetite might be kept on edge for it in the morning. Then she ate other things, with an unwonted zest. Miranda returned to the table, talking pleasantly of everything but health, and food, and hunting. Against herself she was angry; but on Dave, to his surprise, she smiled with a rare graciousness. She was mollified by his tact in characterizing the steak as medicine; and, moreover, by his statement of a preference for their ordinary bloodless table, he seemed in some way to range himself on her side, even while challenging her principles. But—oh, that savoury smell! It still enriched the air of the cabin; it still stirred riotous cravings in her astonished appetite. She trembled with a fear and hatred of herself.

When Kirstie, with a face to which the old glow was already venturing back, laid down her knife and fork, and explained to her guest, "You're a good doctor, and no mistake, Dave Titus; I declare I feel better already," Miranda got up and went silently out into the moonlight to breathe new air and take counsel with herself.

Dave would have followed her, but Kirstie stopped him. "Best let her be," she said meaningly, in a low voice. "She's got a heap to think over in the last half hour."

"But she took it a sight better'n I thought she would," responded Dave.

And all on account of a venison steak, his hopes soared higher than they had ever dared before.

Chapter XVI

Death for a Little Life

THENCEFORWARD Kirstie twice or thrice a week medicined herself with fresh venison, provided assiduously by Young Dave, and by the time spring was fairly in possession of the clearing, she was her old strong self again. But as for Dave's hopes, they had been reduced to desolation. Miranda had taken alarm at her sudden carnivorous craving, and in her effort to undo that moment's weakness she had withdrawn herself to the utmost from Dave's influence. She had been the further incited to this by an imagined aloofness on the part of her furred and feathered pensioners. A pair of foxes, doubtless vagrants from beyond her sphere, had spread slaughter among the hares as they returned from feeding at the cabin. The hungry raiders had laid an ambush at the edge of the clearing on two successive nights. They had killed recklessly. Then they vanished, doubtless driven away by the steady residents who knew how to kill discreetly and to guard their preserves from poachers. But the hares had taken alarm, and few came now o' nights for Miranda's carrots and clover. Miranda, with a little ache at her heart, concluded from this that she had forfeited her ascendency among the kin of the ancient wood. There had been a migration, too, among the squirrels, so that now these red busybodies were perceptibly fewer about the cabin roof. And the birds — they were nearly all gone. An unusually early spring, laying bare the fields in the lower country, and bringing out the insects before their wont, had scattered Miranda's flocks a fortnight earlier than usual. No crumbs could take the place of swelling seeds and the first fat May-fly. But Miranda thought they were fled through distrust of her. Kroof, old Kroof the constant, was all unchanged when she came from her winter's sleep; but this spring she brought an unusually fine cub with her, and the cub, of necessity, took a good deal of her time and attention away from Miranda. When Miranda was with her, roaming the still, transparent corridors, all the untroubled past came back, crystalline and flawless as of old. Once more the furtive folk went about their business in the secure peace of her neighbourhood; once more she revelled with a kind of intoxication in the miraculous fineness of her vision; once more she felt assured of the mastery of her look. But this was in the intervals between Dave's visits. When he was at the clearing, everything was different. She was no longer sure of herself on any point. And the worst of it was that the more indifference to him she feigned, the less she felt. She was quite unconscious, all the while, that her mother was shrewdly watching her struggles. She was not unconscious, however, of Dave's attitude. She saw that he seemed dull and worried, which gratified her, she knew not why, and confirmed her in her coolness. But at last, with a slow anger beginning to burn at his heart, he adopted the policy of ignoring her altogether, and giving all his thought to Kirstie, whereupon Miranda awoke to the conclusion that it was her plain duty to be civil to her mother's guest.

This change, not obtrusive, but of great moment to Dave, came over the girl in June, when the dandelions were starring the pasture grass. The sowing and the potato planting were just done. The lilac bushes beside the cabin were a mass of purple enchantment. It was not a time for hard indifference; and Dave was quick to catch the melting mood. His manner was such, however, that Miranda could not take alarm.

"Mirandy," said he, with the merest good comradeship in tone and air, "would ye take a little trip with me to-morrow, now that the crops can spare ye a bit?"

"Where to, Dave?" interposed Kirstie, fearful lest the girl should refuse out of hand, before she knew what Dave proposed to do.

"Why, I've got to go over the divide an' run down the Big Fork in my canoe to Gabe White's clearin', with some medicine I've brought from the Settlement for his little boy what's sick. He's a leetle mite of a chap, five year old, with long, yaller curls, purty as a picture, but that peaked an' thin, it goes to yer heart to see him. Gabe came in to the Settlement yesterday to see the doctor about him an' git medicine; but he's had to go right on to the city to sell his pelts, an' git some stuff the doctor says the little feller must hev, what can't be got in the Settlement at all. So Gabe give me this" (and he pulled a bottle out of the inside pocket of his hunting shirt) "to take to him right now, coz the little feller needs it badly. It's a right purty trip, Mirandy, an' the Big Fork's got some rapids 'at'll please ye. What ye say?"

Dave was growing subtle under Miranda's discipline. He knew that the picture of the small boy would draw her; and also that the sight of the ailing child, acting upon her quick sympathies, would awaken a new human interest and work secretly in favour of himself. The beauty of the scenery, the excitement of the rapids, — these were a secondary influence, yet he knew they would not be without appeal to the beauty-worshipping and fearless Miranda.

The girl's deep eyes lightened at the prospect. She would see something a little different, yet not alien or hostile, — a new river, other hills and woods, a deeper valley, a ruder cabin in a remoter clearing, a lonely woman, — above all, a little sick boy with long, yellow hair.

"But it must be a long way off, Dave," she protested, in a tone that invited contradiction.

"Not so fur as to the Settlement," answered Dave; "an' it don't take half so long to go because o' the quick run down river. I reckon, though, we'd best stay over night at White's clearin' and come back easy nex' day — if you don't mind, Kirstie! Sary Ann White's a powerful fine woman, an' Mirandy's sure to like her. It'll do her a sight of good, poor thing, to hev Mirandy to talk to a bit."

He wanted to say that just a look at Miranda's wild loveliness would do Mrs. White a lot of good; but he had not quite the courage for such a bold compliment.

"No, I don't mind, if Miranda likes to go," said Kirstie; "I shan't be lonesome, as Kroof'll be round most of the time."

It had come to be understood, and accepted without comment, that when Dave went anywhere with Miranda the jealous old bear remained at home.

Until they were fairly off, Dave was in a fever of anxiety lest Miranda should change her mind. But this venture had genuinely caught her interest, and no whim tempted her to withdraw. After a breakfast eaten so early that the early June dawn was still throwing its streaks of cool red through the cabin window and discouraging the fire upon the hearth, Dave and Miranda set out. They followed the path to the spring among the alders, and then plunged direct into the woods, aiming a little to the east of north. The dew was thick in silver globules on the chips of the yard and on the plantain leaves. It beaded the slender grasses about the spring, and the young foliage of the alders, and the dazzling veils of the gossamer spiders. This time Dave took his rifle with him, and Miranda paid no heed to it.

The woods were drenching wet, but unusually pervaded with light. The new risen sun sent its fresh rays far up the soundless vistas, and every damp leaf or shining facet of bark diffused its little dole of lustre to thin the gloom. As the sun got higher and the dew exhaled away, the twilight slightly deepened, the inexpressible clarity of the shadowed air returned, and the heart of the ancient wood resumed its magic. The awe, as of an enchantment working unseen, the meaning and expectant stillness, the confusion of near and far, the unreality of the familiar,—all this gripped the imagination of the two travellers just as sharply as if they had not been all their lives accustomed to it. The mystery of the ancient wood was not to be staled by use. These two, sensitive to its spell as a surface of glass to a breath, lay open to it in every nerve, and a tense silence fell upon their lips. In the silence was understanding of each other. It was Dave's most potent wooing, against which Miranda had no warning, no defence.

As they walked thus noiselessly, light-footed as the furtive folk themselves, suddenly from a bit of open just ahead of them there came the slender, belling cry of a young deer. They had arrived now, after three hours' rapid walking, at a part of the forest unknown to Miranda. The open space was rock thinly covered with mosses and vines, an upthrust of the granite foundations of a hill which towered near by.

It was an unheard-of thing for a young deer to give cry so heedlessly amid the perilous coverts of the wood. Both the travellers instinctively paused, and then stole forward with greater caution, peering through the branches. To the forest dwellers, beast or human, the unusual is always the suspicious, and therefore to be investigated. A few paces carried them both to a point where Miranda caught sight of the imprudent youngling.

"Hush!" she whispered, laying her hand on Dave's arm. "Look! the poor little thing's lost. Don't frighten it!"

"There'll be something else'll frighten it afore long," muttered Dave, "if it don't quit its bla'tin'."

The words were hardly out of his mouth when the little animal jumped, trembled, started to run, and then looked piteously from side to side, as if uncertain which way to flee and from what peril. An instant more and the greyish-brown form of a lynx shot like lightning from the underbrush. It caught the young deer by the throat, dragged it down, tore it savagely, and began drinking its blood.

"Kill it! kill it!" panted Miranda, starting forward. But Dave's hand checked her.

"Wait!" he said firmly. "The little critter's dead; we can't do it no good. Wait an' we'll git both the varmints. There'll be a pair of 'em."

Under ordinary circumstances, Miranda would have resented the idea of getting "both the varmints"; but just now she was savage with pity for the young deer, and she chose to remember vindictively that far-off day when Ganner had come to the clearing, and only the valour of Star, the brindled ox, had saved herself and Michael, the calf, from a cruel death. She obeyed Dave's command, therefore, and waited.

But there was another who would not wait. The mother doe had heard her lost little one's appeal. In wild haste, but noiseless on the deep carpet of the moss, she came leaping to the cry. She saw what Miranda and Dave saw. But she did not pause to calculate, or weigh the odds against her. With one bound she was out in the open. With the next she was upon the destroyer. The hungry lynx looked up just in time to avoid the fair impact of her descending hooves, which would have broken his back. As it was, he caught a glancing blow on the flank, which ripped his fine fur and hurled him several paces down the slope.

Before he could fully recover, the deer was upon him again; and Miranda, her eyes glowing, her cheeks scarlet with excitement and exultation, clutched her companion's arm with such a grip that her slim fingers hurt him deliciously. The lynx, alarmed and furious, twisted himself over and fixed both claws and teeth in his adversary's leg, just below the shoulder. Fierce and strong as he was, he was nevertheless getting badly punished, when his mate appeared bounding down the slope, and with a sharp snarl sprang upon the doe's neck, bearing her to her knees.

"Shoot! shoot!" cried Miranda, springing away from Dave's side to give him room. But his rifle was at his shoulder ere she spoke. With the word his shot rang out; and the second assailant dropped to the ground, kicking. Immediately Dave ran forward. The male lynx, disentangling himself, darted for cover; but just as he was disappearing, Dave gave him the second barrel, at short range, and the bullet caught him obliquely across the hind quarters, breaking his spine. Dave was noted as the best shot in all that region; but the marksmanship which he had just displayed was lost on Miranda. She took it for granted that to shoot was to hit, and to hit was to kill, as a matter of course. Dave's first shot had killed. The animal was already motionless. But the writhings of the other lynx, prone in the bush, tore her heart.

"Oh, how it's suffering! Kill it, quick!" she panted. Dave ran up, swung his rifle in a short grip, and struck the beast a settling blow at the base of the skull. The deer, meanwhile, limping and bleeding, but not seriously the worse for her dreadful encounter, hobbled back to where the body of her young lay stretched upon the moss. She sniffed at it for a moment with her delicate nose, satisfied herself that it was quite dead, then moved off slowly into the shadows.

Miranda went to each of the three slain animals in turn, and looked at them thoughtfully, while Dave waited in silence, uncertain what to do next. He felt that it behooved him to step warily while Miranda was wrestling with emotions.

At last she said, with a sob in her voice, and her eyes very bright and large, —

"Come, let's get away from this horrid place!"

Dave experienced a certain mild pang at the thought of leaving two good pelts behind him to be gnawed by foxes; but he followed Miranda without a word. It would have been a fatal error to talk of furs at that moment. As soon, however, as they were out of sight of the open slope, he turned aside and headed their course toward a rocky knoll which was visible through the trees.

"What are you going that way for?" asked Miranda.

"Likely the lou'-cerfies had their den in the rocks yonder," was the reply; "we must find it."

"What do we want of their den?" queried the girl in surprise.

"There'll be a couple of lou'-cerfie kittens in it, I reckon," said Dave, "an' we must find 'em."

"What for?" demanded Miranda, suspiciously.

Dave looked at her.

"You've had me shoot the father an' mother, Mirandy," he said slowly, "for the sake of the deer. An' now would ye hev the little ones starve to death?"

"I never thought of that, Dave," answered the girl, smitten with remorse; and she looked at him with a new approval. She thought to herself that he, hunter and blood-stained as he was, showed yet a readier and more reasonable tenderness for the furry kindred than she herself.

For nearly half an hour they searched the hollows of the rocky knoll, and at last came upon a shallow cave overhung darkly by a mat of dwarf cedar. There were bones about the entrance, and inside, upon a bed of dry moss, were two small rusty brown, kitten-like objects curled softly together. Miranda's discerning vision perceived them at once, but it took Dave's eyes some seconds to adapt themselves to the gloom. Then the furry ball of "lou'-cerfie" kittens looked to him very pretty — something to be fondled and protected. He knew well how their helplessness would appeal to Miranda's tender heart. Nevertheless, with a firmness of courage which, under the circumstances, few heroes would have arisen to, he stepped forward, stooped, untangled the soft ball, and with the heavy handle of his hunting-knife struck each kitten just one sharp stroke on the neck, killing it instantly and easily.

"Poor little critters!" he muttered; "it was the only thing to do with 'em," and he turned to Miranda.

The girl had backed out of the cave and now stood, with flushed face, staring at him fiercely.

"You brute!" she exclaimed.

Dave had been prepared for some discussion of his action. But he was not prepared for just this. He drew himself up.

"I did think ye was a woman grown; an' for all yer idees were kind of far-fetched, I've respected 'em a heap; an' I won't say but what they've influenced me, too. But now I see ye're but a silly child an' don't reason. Did ye think, maybe, these here leetle mites o' things could live an' take keer o' themselves?"

He spoke coldly, scornfully; and there was a kind of mastery in his voice that quelled her. She was astonished, too. The colour in her face deepened, but she dropped her eyes.

"I wanted to take them home, and tame them," she explained, quite humbly.

Dave's stern face softened.

"Ye'd never 'a' been able to raise 'em. They're too young, a sight too young. See, their eyes ain't open. They'd have jest died on yer hands, Mirandy, sure an' sartain!"

"But—how *could* you!" she protested, with no more anger left, but a sob of pity in her throat.

"It was jest what *you* do to the fish ye ketch, Mirandy, to stop their sufferin'."

Miranda looked up quickly, and her eyes grew large.

"Do you know, I never thought of that before, Dave," she replied. "I'll never catch a fish again, long as I live! Let's get away from here."

"Ye see," began Dave, making up his mind to sow a few seeds of doubt in Miranda's mind as to the correctness of her theories, "ye see, Mirandy, 't ain't possible to be consistent right through in this life; but what ye'll find, life'll make a fool o' ye at one point or another. I ain't a-goin' to say I think ye're all wrong, not by no means. Sence I've seen the way ye understand the live critters of the woods, an' how they understand you, I've come to feel some different about killin' 'em myself. But, Mirandy, Nature's nature, an' ye can't do much by buckin' up agin her. Look now, ye told me to shoot the lou'-cerfie coz he killed the deer kid. But he didn't go to kill it for ugliness, nor jest for himself to make a dinner off of — you know that. He killed it for his mate, too. Lou'-cerfie ain't built so's they can eat grass. If the she lou'-cerfie didn't git the meat she needed, her kittens'd starve. She's jest *got* to kill. Nature's put that law onto her, an' onto the painters, an' the foxes an' wolves, the 'coons an' the weasels.

An' she's put the same law, only not so heavy, onto the bears, an' also onto humans, what's all built to live on all kinds of food, meat among the rest. An' to live right, and be their proper selves, they've all got to eat meat sometimes, for Nature don't stand much foolin' with her laws!"

"*I'm* well," interrupted Miranda, eagerly, with the obvious retort.

"Maybe ye won't be always!" suggested Dave.

"Then I'll be sick — then I'll *die* before I'll eat meat!" she protested passionately. "What's the good of living, anyway, if it's nothing but kill, kill, kill, and for one that lives a lot have got to die!"

Dave shook his head soberly.

"That's what nobody, fur's I can see, Mirandy, has ever been able to make out yet. I've thought about it a heap, an' read about it a heap, alone in camp, an' I can't noways see through it. Oftentimes it's seemed to me all life was jest like a few butterflies flitterin' over a graveyard.

But all the same, if we don't go to too much foolish worryin' 'bout what we can't understand, we do feel it's good to be alive; an' I do think, Mirandy, this life *might* be somethin' finer than the finest kind of a dream."

Something in his voice, at these last words, thrilled Miranda, and at the same time put her on her guard.

"Well," she exclaimed positively, if not relevantly, "I'm never going to catch another fish."

The answer not being just what Dave needed for the support of his advance, he lost courage, and let the conversation drop.

Chapter XVII

In the Roar of the Rapids

A LITTLE before noon, when the midsummer heat of the outside world came filtering faintly down even into the cool vistas of the forest, and here and there a pale-blue butterfly danced with his mate across the clear shadow, and the aromatic wood smells came out more abundantly than was their wont, at the lure of the persuasive warmth, the travellers halted for noonmeat. Sitting on a fallen hemlock trunk beside a small but noisy brook, it was a frugal meal they made on the cheese and dark bread which Kirstie had put in Dave's satchel. Their halt was brief; and as they set out again, Dave said: —

"'T ain't a mile from here to the Big Fork. Gabe's canoe's hid in the bushes just where this here brook falls in. Noisy, ain't it?"

"I love the sound," exclaimed Miranda, stepping quickly and gaily, as if the light, musical clamour of the stream had got into her blood.

"Well, the Big Fork's a sight noisier," continued Dave. "It's heavy water, an' just rapids on rapids all the ways down to Gabe's clearing. Ye won't be skeered, Mirandy?"

The girl gave one of her rare laughs, very high-pitched, but brief, musical, and curiously elusive. She was excited at the prospect.

"I reckon you know how to handle a canoe, Dave," was all she said. The trust in her voice made Dave feel measurably nearer his purpose. He durst not speak, lest his elation should betray itself.

In a little while there came another sound, not drowning or even obscuring the clear prattle of the brook, but serving as a heavy background to its brightness. It was a large, yet soft, pulsating thunder, and seemed to come from all sides at once; as if far-off herds, at march over hollow lands, were closing in upon them. Dave looked at Miranda. She gave him a shining glance of comprehension.

"It's the rapids!" she cried. "Do we go through those?"

Dave laughed.

"Not those! Not by a long chalk! That's the 'Big Soo' ye hear, an' it's more a fall than a rapid. Ther's an eddy an' a still water jest below, an' that's where we take to the canoe."

As they went on, the great swelling noise seemed to Miranda to fill her soul, and worked a deep yet still excitement within her. Nevertheless, rapidly as its volume increased, the light chatter of the brook was upborne distinctly upon the flood of it. Then, suddenly, as the forest thinned ahead, and the white daylight confronted them, the voice of the brook was in an instant overwhelmed, utterly effaced. The softly pervasive thunder burst all at once into a trembling roar, vehement, conflicting, explosive; and they came out full in face of a long, distorted slope of cataract White, yellow, tawny green, the waves bounded and wallowed down the loud steep; and here and there the black bulks of rock shouldered upward, opposing them eternally.

Spellbound at the sight, Miranda stood gazing, while Dave fetched from the bushes a ruddy-yellow canoe of birch bark, and launched it in a quiet but foam-flecked back-water at their feet. In the bow he placed a compact bundle of bracken for Miranda to sit upon, with another flat bundle at her back, that the cross-bar might not gall her.

"Best fer ye to sit low, Mirandy, 'stead o' kneelin'," he explained, "coz I'll be standin' up, with the pole, goin' through some o' the rips, an' ye'll be steadier sittin' than kneelin'."

"But I paddle better kneeling," protested Miranda.

"Ye won't need to paddle," said Dave, a little grimly. "Ye'll jest maybe fend a rock now an' agin, that's all. The current an' me'll do the rest."

The fall of the "Big Soo" ended in a basin very wide and deep, whose spacious caverns absorbed the fury of the waters and allowed them to flow off sullenly. Dave knelt in the stern, paddle in hand, and the long pole of white spruce sticking out behind the canoe, where he could lay his grasp upon it in an instant. A couple of strokes sent the little craft out into the smooth, purplish-amber swirls of the deep current, whereon the froth clusters wheeled slowly. A few minutes more and a green fringed overhang of rock was rounded, the last energy of the current spent itself in a deep and roomy channel, the uproar of the cataract mellowed suddenly to that pulsating thunder which they had heard at first, and the canoe, under Dave's noiseless propulsion, shot forward over a surface as of dark brown glass. There was a mile of this still water, along which Miranda insisted upon paddling. The rocks rose straight from the channel, and the trees hung down from their rim, and the June sun, warmly flooding the trough of rock and water, made its grimness greatly beautiful. Then the rocks diminished, and the steep, richly green slopes of the hillsides came down to the water's edge, and a rushing clamour began to swell in the distance. The currents awakened under the canoe, which darted forward more swiftly. The shouting of the "rips" seemed to rush up stream to meet them. The surface of the river began to slant away before them, not breaking yet, but furrowing into long, thready streaks. Then, far down the slant, a tossing white line of short breakers, drawn right across the channel, clambered toward them ravenously.

"Ye'd better not paddle now, Mirandy," said Dave, in a quiet voice, standing up for a moment to survey the channel, while the canoe slipped swiftly down toward the turmoil. "There's rapids now all the way down to Gabe's clearing. An' we won't be long goin', neither."

A moment more, and to Miranda it seemed that the leafy shores ran by her, that the gnashing phalanx of the waves sprang up at her. She had never run a rapid before. Her experience of canoeing had all been gained on the lake. She caught her breath, but did not flinch as the tumbling waters seethed and yammered around her. Then her blood ran hot with the excitement of it; her nerves tingled. She wanted to cry out, to paddle wildly and fiercely. But she held herself under curb. She never moved. Only the grip of her hands on the paddle, which lay idle before her, tightened till the knuckles went white. There was no word from Dave; no sign of his presence save that the canoe shot straight as an arrow, and bit firmly upon the big surges, so that she knew his wrist of steel was in control. Suddenly, just ahead, sprang a square black rock, against which the mad rush of water upreared and fell back broken to either side. The canoe leaped straight at it, and Miranda held her breath.

"Stroke on the right!" came Dave's sharp order. She dipped her paddle strenuously, twice — thrice — and, swerving at the last moment, while the currents seethed up along her bulwarks, the canoe darted safely past.

Miranda stopped paddling. There was a steeper slope in front, but a clear channel, the waves not high but wallowing inward toward the centre. Straight down this centre rushed the canoe, the surges clutching at her on both sides, yellow green, with white foam-streaks veining their very hearts. At the foot of the slope, singing sharply and shining in the sun, curved a succession of three great "ripples," stationary in mid-channel, their back-curled crests thin and prismatic. Straight through these Dave steered. The three thin crests, thus swiftly divided, one after another, slapped Miranda coldly in the face, drenching her, and leaving a good bucketful of water in the canoe.

"Oh!" gasped Miranda, at the shock, and shook her hair, laughing excitedly.

There was gentler water now for a hundred yards or so, and Dave steered cautiously for shore.

"We'll hev to land an' empty her out," said he. "Ther's no more big 'ripples' like them there on the whole river; an' we won't take in water agin 'twixt here an' Gabe's."

"I don't care if we do!" exclaimed

Miranda, fervently. "It was splendid, Dave! And you did it just fine!"

This commendation took him aback somewhat, and he was unable to show his appreciation of it except by a foolish grin, which remained on his face while he turned the canoe over and while he launched it again. It was still there when Miranda resumed her place in the bow; and, strangely enough, she felt no disposition to criticise him for it.

The rest of the journey, lasting nearly an hour longer, was a ceaseless succession of rapids, with scant and few spaces of quiet water between. None were quite so long and violent as the first; but by the time the canoe slowed up in the reach of still water that ran through the interval meadow of Gabe's clearing, Miranda felt fagged from the long-sustained excitement. She felt as if it had been she, not Dave, whose unerring eye and unfailing wrist had brought the canoe in triumph through the menace of the roaring races.

They landed on the blossoming meadow strip, and Dave turned the canoe over among the grasses, under the shade of an elm that would serve to keep the afternoon sun from melting the rosin off the seams. Gabe's cabin stood a stone's throw back from the meadow, high enough up the slope to be clear of the spring freshets. It was a bare, uncared-for place, with black stumps still dotting all the fields of buckwheat and potatoes, a dishevelled-looking barn, and no vine or bush about the house. It gave Miranda a pang of pity to look at it. Her own cabin was lonely enough, but with a high, austere, clear loneliness that seemed to hold communion with the stars. The loneliness of this place was a shut-in, valley loneliness, without horizons and without hope. She felt sorry almost to tears for the white and sad-eyed woman who appeared in the cabin door to welcome them.

"Sary Ann, this is Mirandy I spoke to ye about."

The two women shook hands somewhat shyly, and, after the silent fashion of their race, said nothing.

"How's Jimmy?" asked Dave.

"'Baout the same, thank ye, Dave," replied the woman, wearily, leading the way into the cabin.

In a low chair near the window, playing listlessly with a dingy red-and-yellow rag doll, sat a thin-faced, pallid little boy with long, pale curls down on his shoulders. He lifted sorrowful blue eyes to Miranda's face, as she, with a swift impulse of tenderness and compassion, rushed forward and knelt down to embrace him. Her vitality and the loving brightness of her look won the child at once. His wan little face lightened. He lifted the baby mouth to be kissed. Miranda pressed his fair head to her bosom gently, and had much ado to keep her eyes from running over, so worked the love and pity and the mothering hunger in her heart.

"He takes to ye, Mirandy," said the woman, smiling upon her. And Dave, his passion almost mastering him, blurted out proudly, —

"An' who wouldn't take to her, I'd like to know?"

He felt at this moment that Miranda was

now all human, and could never quite go back to her mystic and uncanny wildness, her preference for the speechless, furry kin over her own warm, human kind. He produced the medicine from his satchel; and from Miranda's attentive hand Jimmy took the stuff as if it had been nectar. Jimmy's mother looked on with undisguised approval of the girl. Had she thought Miranda was going to stay any length of time, her mother-jealousy would have been aroused; but as it was she was only exquisitely relieved at the thought of Jimmy's being in some one else's care for a few hours. She whispered audibly — a mere chaffing pretence of a whisper it was — to Dave: —

"It's a right purty an' a right smart little wife she'll make fer ye, Dave Titus, an' she'll know how to mind yer babies. Ye're a lucky man, an' I hope ye understand how lucky ye air!"

Poor Dave! She might as well have thrown a bucket of cold water in his face. For an instant he could have strangled the kindly, coarse-grained, well-meaning, silly woman, who stood beaming her pale goodwill upon them both. He cursed himself for not having warned her that Miranda could not be chaffed like a common Settlement girl. He saw Miranda's face go scarlet to the ears, though she bent over Jimmy and pretended to have heard nothing; and he knew that in that moment his good work was all undone. For a few seconds he could say nothing, and the silence grew trying. Then he stammered out:—

"I'm afeard ther's no sich luck fer me, Sary Ann, though God knows I want her. But Mirandy don't like me very well."

The woman stared at him incredulously.

"Lord sakes, Dave Titus, then what's she doin' here alone with you?" she exclaimed, the weariness coming back into her voice at the last of the phrase. "Oh, you go 'long! You don't know nothin' about women!"

This was quite too much for Dave, whose instincts, fined by long months in the companionship of only the great trees, the great winds, and the grave stars, had grown unerringly delicate. His own face flushed up now for Miranda's sake.

"I'd take it kindly of ye, Sary Ann, if ye'd quit the subject right there," he said quietly. But there was a firmness in his voice which the woman understood.

"The both of ye must be nigh dead for somethin' to eat," she said. "I must git ye supper right off." And she turned to the fireplace and filled the kettle.

Thereafter, through supper, and through the short evening, Miranda had never a word for Dave. She talked a little, kindly and without showing her resentment, to Mrs. White; but her attentions were entirely absorbed in little Jimmy. Indeed, she had Jimmy very much to herself, for Mrs. White got Dave to help with the chores and the milking. Afterward, about the hearth-fire, — maintained for its cheer and not for warmth, — Mrs. White confined her conversation largely to Dave. She was not angry at him on account of his rebuke — but vaguely aggrieved at Miranda as the cause of it. She began to feel that Miranda was different from other girls, from what she herself had been as a girl. Miranda's fineness and sensitiveness were something of an offence to her, though she could not define them at all. She characterized them vaguely by the phrase "stuck up"; and became presently inclined to think that a fine fellow like Dave was too good for her. Still, she was a fair-minded woman in her worn, colourless way; and she could not but allow there must be a lot in Miranda if little Jimmy took to her so — "For a child knows a good heart," she said to herself.

Next morning, soon after dawn, the travellers were off, Miranda tearing herself with difficulty from little Jimmy's embrace, and leaving him in a desolation of tears. She was quite civil and ordinary with Dave now, so much so that good, obtuse, weary Mrs. White concluded that all was at rights again. But Dave felt the icy difference; and he was too proud, if not for the time too hopeless, to try to thaw it. During all the long, laborious journey upward through the rapids, by poling, he did wonders of skill and strength, but in utter silence. His feats were not lost upon Miranda, but she hardened her heart resolutely; for now a shame, which she had never known before, gave tenacity to her anger. Through it all, however, she couldn't help thrilling to the strife with the loud rapids, and exulting in the slow, inexorable conquest of them. The return march through the woods was in the main a silent one, as before; but how different a silence! Not electric with meaning, but cold, the silence of a walled chamber. And, as if the spirits of the wood maliciously enjoyed Dave's discomfiture, they permitted no incident, no diversion. They kept the wood-folk all away, they emptied of all life and significance the forest spaces. And Dave grew sullen.

Arriving back at the clearing just before sundown, they paused at the cabin door. Dave looked into Miranda's eyes with something of reproach, something of appeal. Kirstie's voice, talking cheerfully to Kroof, came from the raspberry brambles behind the house. Miranda stretched out her hand with a cool frankness, and returned his look blankly.

"I've had a real good time, thank you, Dave," she said. "You'll find mother yonder, picking raspberries."

Chapter XVIII

The Forfeit of the Alien

ALL through the summer and early autumn Dave continued his fortnightly visits to the cabin in the clearing, and always Miranda treated him with the same cold, casual civility. She felt, or pretended to herself that she felt, grateful now to the blunt-fingered, wan woman over at Gabe White's, who had rudely jostled her back to her senses when she was on the very edge of giving up her freedom and her personality to a man — a strong man, who would have absorbed her. She flung herself passionately once more into the fellowship of the furtive folk, the secrecy and wonder of the wood. As it was a human love which she was crushing out, and as she felt the need of humanity cravingly, though not understandingly, at her heart, she lavished upon

Kirstie a demonstrativeness of affection such as she had never shown before. It pleased Kirstie, and she met it heartily in her calm, strong way; but she saw through it, and smiled at the back of her brain, scarcely daring to think her thought frankly, lest the girl's intuition should discern it. She made much of Dave, but never before Miranda; and she kept encouraging the rather despondent man with the continual assertion: "It'll be all right, Dave. Don't fret, but bide your time." To which Dave responded by biding his time with a quiet, unaggressive persistence; and if he fretted, he took pains not to show it.

If Dave had an ally in Kirstie, he had consistent antagonists in all the folk of the wood; for never before in all Miranda's semi-occult experience had the folk of the wood come so near to her. Kroof was her almost ceaseless companion, more devoted, if possible, than ever, and certainly more quick in comprehension of Miranda's English. And Kroof's cub, a particularly fine and well-grown young animal, was well-nigh as devoted as his mother. When these two were absent on some rare expedition of their own, undertaken by Kroof for the hardening of the cub's muscles, then the very foxes took to following Miranda, close to heel, like dogs; and one drowsy fall afternoon, when she had lain down to sleep on a sloping patch of pine needles, the selfsame big panther from whom she had rescued Dave came lazily and lay down beside her. His large purring at her ear awoke her. He purred still more loudly when she gently scratched him under the throat. She was filled with a curious exaltation as she marked how her influence over the wild things grew and widened. Nothing, she vowed, should ever lure her away from these clear shades, these silent folks whom she ruled by hand and eye, and this mysterious life which she alone could know. When Old Dave, for whom she cared warmly, made his now infrequent visits to the clearing, she had an inclination to avoid him, lest he should attack her purpose; and the thought of little Jimmy's white face and baby mouth she put away obstinately, as most dangerous of all. And so it came that when October arrived, and all the forest everywhere was noiselessly astir with falling leaves, and the light of the blue began to peer in upon the places which had been closed to it all summer, by that time Miranda felt quite secure in her resolve; and Dave's fight now was to keep the despair of his heart from writing itself large upon his face.

Toward the end of that October Dave's hunting took him to the rocky open ground where, in the previous June, he and Miranda had encountered the lynxes. He was looking for fresh meat for Kirstie, and game, that day, had kept aloof. Just as he recognized, with a kind of homesick ache of remembrance, the spot where he and Miranda had seemed, for a brief space, to be in perfect accord with each other, — how long ago and how unbelievable it appeared to him now! — his hunter's eye caught a sight which brought the rifle to his shoulder. Just at the edge of the open a young bear stood greedily stripping blueberries from the laden bushes, and grunting with satisfaction at the sweet repast.

"A bit of bear steak," thought Dave, "will be jest the thing for Kirstie. She's gittin' a mite tired o' deer's meat!"

An unhurried aim, a sharp, slapping report, and the handsome cub sank forward upon his snout, and rolled over, shot through the brain. Dave strode up to him. He had died instantly — so instantly and painlessly that his half-open mouth was still full of berries and small, dark green leaves. Dave felt his soft and glossy dark coat.

"Ye're a fine young critter," he muttered half regretfully. "It was kind o' mean to cut ye off when ye was havin' such a good time all to yerself."

But Dave was not one to nurse an idle sentimentality. Without delay he skinned the carcase, and *cached* the pelt carefully under a pile of heavy stones, intending to return for it the first day possible. He was going to the clearing now, and could not take a raw pelt with him, to damn him finally in Miranda's eyes; but the skin was too fine a one to be left to the foxes and wolverines. When it was safely bestowed, he cut off the choicest portions of the carcase, wrapped them in leaves and tied them up in birch bark, slung the package over his shoulder, and set out in haste for the clearing. He was anxious that Kirstie should have bear steaks for supper that night.

He had been but a little while gone from the rocky open, where the red carcase lay hideously affronting the sunlight, when another bear emerged in leisurely fashion from the shadows. It was an animal of huge size and with rusty fur that was greying about the snout. She paused to look around her. On the instant her body stiffened, and then she went crashing through the blueberry bushes to where that dreadful thing lay bleeding. She walked around it twice, with her nose in the air, and again with her nose to the ground. Then she backed away from it slowly down the slope, her stare fixed upon it as if she expected it might rise and follow. At the edge of the wood she wheeled quickly, and went at a savage gallop along the trail which Dave had taken.

It was old Kroof; and Dave had killed her cub.

She rushed on madly, a terrible avenger of blood; but so fast was Dave journeying that it was not much short of an hour before her instinct or some keen sense told her that he was close at hand. She was not blinded by her fury. Rather was she coolly and deliberately set upon a sufficing vengeance. She moderated her pace, and went softly; and soon she caught sight of her quarry some way ahead, striding swiftly down the brown-shadowed vistas.

There was no other bear in all the forests so shrewd as Kroof; and she knew that for the hunter armed all her tremendous strength and fury were no match. She waited to catch him at a disadvantage. Her huge bulk kept the trail as noiselessly as a weasel or a mink. Young Dave, with all his woodcraft, all his alertness of sense, all his intuition, had no guess of the dark Nemesis which was so inexorably dogging his stride. He was in such haste that in spite of the autumn chill his hair clung moistly to his forehead. When he reached the rivulet flowing away from the cabin spring, he felt that he must have a wash-up before presenting himself. Under a big hemlock he dropped his bundle, threw off his cap, his belt, his shirt, and laid down his loaded rifle. Then, bare to the waist, he went on some twenty paces to a spot where the stream made a convenient pool, and knelt down to give himself a thorough freshening.

Kroof's little eyes gleamed redly. Here was her opportunity.

She crept forward, keeping the trunk of the hemlock between herself and her foe, till she reached the things which Dave had thrown down under the tree. She sniffed at the rolled-up package and turned it over with her paw. Then, with one short, grunting cough of rage and pain, she launched herself upon the murderer of her cub.

That savage cry was Dave's first hint of danger. He looked up quickly, his head and shoulders dripping. He recognized Kroof. There was no time for choice. The huge animal was just upon him; but in that instant he understood the whole tragedy. His heart sickened. There was a great beech tree just across the pool, almost within arm's length. With one bound he reached it. With the next he caught a branch and swung himself up, just eluding the vengeful sweep of Kroof's paw.

Nimbly he mounted, seeking a branch which would lead him to another tree and so back to the ground and his rifle; and Kroof, after a moment's pause, climbed after him. But Dave could not find what he sought. Few were the trees in the ancient wood whose topmost branches did not twine closely with their neighbour trees. But with a man's natural aversion to bathing in water that is not enlivened and inspirited by the direct sunlight, Dave had chosen a spot where the trees were scattered and the blue of the sky looked in. He climbed to a height of some forty or fifty feet from the ground before he found a branch that seemed to offer any hope at all. Out upon this he stepped, steadying himself by a slenderer branch above his head. Following it as far as the branch would support him, he saw that his position was all but hopeless. He could not, even by the most accurate and fortunate swing, catch the nearest branch of the nearest tree. He turned back, but Kroof was already at the fork. Her claws were already fixed upon the branch; she was crawling out to him slowly, inexorably; she had him in a trap.

Dave stood tense and moveless, awaiting her. His face was white, his mouth set. He knew that in all human probability his hour was come; yet what might be done, he would do. Far below, between him and the mingling of rock and moss which formed the ground (he looked down upon it, chequered with the late sunlight), was a stout hemlock branch. At the last moment he would drop; and the branch — he would clutch at it —

might perhaps break his fall, at least in part. It was a meagre chance, but his only one. He was not shaken by fear, but he felt aggrieved and disappointed at such a termination of his hopes; and the deadly irony of his fate stung him. The branch bent lower and lower as Kroof's vast weight drew near. The branch above, too frail to endure his weight alone, still served to steady him. He kept his head erect, challenging death.

It chanced that Miranda, not far off, had heard the roar with which Kroof had rushed to the attack. The fury of it had brought her in haste to the spot, surprised and apprehensive. She recognized Dave's rifle and hunting-shirt under the hemlock tree, and her heart melted in a horrible fear. Then she saw Dave high up in the beech tree, his bare shoulders gleaming through the russet leaves. She saw Kroof, now not three feet from her prey. She saw the hate in the beast's eyes and open jaws.

"Kroof!" she cried, in a tone of fierce command; and Kroof heeded her no more than if she had been the wind whispering.

"Kroof! Kroof!" she cried again, in anguished appeal, in piercing terror, as the savage animal crept on. Dave did not turn his head, but he called down in a quiet voice: "Ye can't do it this time, Mirandy. I guess it's good-by now, for good!"

But Miranda's face had suddenly set itself to stone. She snatched up the rifle. "Hold on!" she cried, and taking a careful, untrembling aim she pulled first one trigger, then the other, in such quick succession that the two reports came almost as one. Then she dropped the weapon, and stood staring wildly.

The bear's body heaved convulsively for a moment, then seemed to fall together on the branch, clutching at it. A second later and it rolled off, with a leisurely motion, and came plunging downward, soft, massive, enormous. It struck the ground with a sobbing thud. Miranda gave a low cry at the sound, turned away, and leaned against the trunk of the hemlock. Her face was toward the tree, and hidden in the bend of her arm.

Dave knew now that all he had hoped for was his. Yet, after the first overwhelming, choking throb of exultation, his heart swelled with pity for the girl, with pity and immeasurable tenderness. He descended from his refuge, put on his hunting-shirt and belt, looked curiously at the empty rifle where it lay on the moss, and kicked the corded package of meat into a thicket. Then he went and stood close beside Miranda.

After a moment or two he laid an arm about her shoulders and touched her with his large hand, lightly firm. "Ye wonderful Mirandy," he said, "you've give me life over agin! I ain't a-goin' to thank ye, though, till I know what ye're goin' to do with me. My life's been jest all yours since first I seen ye a woman grown. What'll ye do with the life ye've saved, Mirandy?"

He pressed her shoulder close against his heart, and leaned over, not quite daring to kiss the bronze-dark hair on which he breathed. The girl turned suddenly, with a sob, and caught hold of him, and hid her face in his breast. "Oh, Dave!" she cried, in a piteous voice, "take mother and me away from this place; I don't want to live at the clearing any more. You've killed the old life I loved." And she broke into a storm of tears.

Dave waited till she was quieter. Then he said: "If I've changed your life, Mirandy, ye've changed mine a sight, too. I'll hunt and trap no more, dear, an' the beasts'll hev no more trouble 'long o' me. We'll sell the clearin', an' go 'way down onto the Meramichi, where I can git a good job surveyin' lumber. I'm right smart at that. An' I reckon — oh, I love ye, an' I need ye, an' I reckon I can make ye happy, ye wonderful Mirandy."

The girl heard him through, then gently released herself from his arms. "You go an' tell mother what I've done, Dave," she said, in a steady voice, "and leave me here a little while with Kroof."

That evening, after Miranda had returned to the cabin, Kirstie and Dave came with spades and a lantern to the beech tree by the pool. Where they could find room in the rocky soil, they dug a grave; and there they buried old Kroof deeply, that neither might the claws of the wolverine disturb her, nor any lure of spring suns waken her from her sleep.

THE NEW CANADIAN LIBRARY

n 1. OVER PRAIRIE TRAILS / Frederick Philip Grove
n 2. SUCH IS MY BELOVED / Morley Callaghan
n 3. LITERARY LAPSES / Stephen Leacock
n 4. AS FOR ME AND MY HOUSE / Sinclair Ross
n 5. THE TIN FLUTE / Gabrielle Roy
n 6. THE CLOCKMAKER / Thomas Chandler Haliburton
n 7. THE LAST BARRIER AND OTHER STORIES / Charles G. D. Roberts
n 8. BAROMETER RISING / Hugh MacLennan
n 9. AT THE TIDE'S TURN AND OTHER STORIES / Thomas H. Raddall
n10. ARCADIAN ADVENTURES WITH THE IDLE RICH / Stephen Leacock
n11. HABITANT POEMS / William Henry Drummond
n12. THIRTY ACRES / Ringuet
n13. EARTH AND HIGH HEAVEN / Gwethalyn Graham
n14. THE MAN FROM GLENGARRY / Ralph Connor
n15. SUNSHINE SKETCHES OF A LITTLE TOWN / Stephen Leacock
n16. THE STEPSURE LETTERS / Thomas McCulloch
n17. MORE JOY IN HEAVEN / Morley Callaghan
n18. WILD GEESE / Martha Ostenso
n19. THE MASTER OF THE MILL / Frederick Philip Grove
n20. THE IMPERIALIST / Sara Jeannette Duncan
n21. DELIGHT / Mazo de la Roche
n22. THE SECOND SCROLL / A. M. Klein
n23. THE MOUNTAIN AND THE VALLEY / Ernest Buckler
n24. THE RICH MAN / Henry Kreisel
n25. WHERE NESTS THE WATER HEN / Gabrielle Roy
n26. THE TOWN BELOW / Roger Lemelin
n27. THE HISTORY OF EMILY MONTAGUE / Frances Brooke
n28. MY DISCOVERY OF ENGLAND / Stephen Leacock
n29. SWAMP ANGEL / Ethel Wilson
n30. EACH MAN'S SON / Hugh MacLennan
n31. ROUGHING IT IN THE BUSH / Susanna Moodie
n32. WHITE NARCISSUS / Raymond Knister
n33. THEY SHALL INHERIT THE EARTH / Morley Callaghan
n34. TURVEY / Earle Birney
n35. NONSENSE NOVELS / Stephen Leacock
n36. GRAIN / R. J. C. Stead
n37. LAST OF THE CURLEWS / Fred Bodsworth
n38. THE NYMPH AND THE LAMP / Thomas H. Raddall
n39. JUDITH HEARNE / Brian Moore
n40. THE CASHIER / Gabrielle Roy
n41. UNDER THE RIBS OF DEATH / John Marlyn
n42. WOODSMEN OF THE WEST / M. Allerdale Grainger
n43. MOONBEAMS FROM THE LARGER LUNACY / Stephen Leacock
n44. SARAH BINKS / Paul Hiebert
n45. SON OF A SMALLER HERO / Mordecai Richler
n46. WINTER STUDIES AND SUMMER RAMBLES / Anna Jameson
n47. REMEMBER ME / Edward Meade
n48. FRENZIED FICTION / Stephen Leacock
n49. FRUITS OF THE EARTH / Frederick Philip Grove
n50. SETTLERS OF THE MARSH / Frederick Philip Grove

n51. THE BACKWOODS OF CANADA / Catharine Parr Traill
n52. MUSIC AT THE CLOSE / Edward McCourt
n53. MY REMARKABLE UNCLE / Stephen Leacock
n54. THE DOUBLE HOOK / Sheila Watson
n55. TIGER DUNLOP'S UPPER CANADA / William Dunlop
n56. STREET OF RICHES / Gabrielle Roy
n57. SHORT CIRCUITS / Stephen Leacock
n58. WACOUSTA / John Richardson
n59. THE STONE ANGEL / Margaret Laurence
n60. FURTHER FOOLISHNESS / Stephen Leacock
n61. MARCHBANKS' ALMANACK / Robertson Davies
n62. THE LAMP AT NOON AND OTHER STORIES / Sinclair Ross
n63. THE HARBOUR MASTER / Theodore Goodridge Roberts
n64. THE CANADIAN SETTLER'S GUIDE / Catharine Parr Traill
n65. THE GOLDEN DOG / William Kirby
n66. THE APPRENTICESHIP OF DUDDY KRAVITZ / Mordecai Richler
n67. BEHIND THE BEYOND / Stephen Leacock
n68. A STRANGE MANUSCRIPT FOUND IN A COPPER CYLINDER / James De Mille
n69. LAST LEAVES / Stephen Leacock
n70. THE TOMORROW-TAMER / Margaret Laurence
n71. ODYSSEUS EVER RETURNING / George Woodcock
n72. THE CURÉ OF ST. PHILIPPE / Francis William Grey
n73. THE FAVOURITE GAME / Leonard Cohen
n74. WINNOWED WISDOM / Stephen Leacock
n75. THE SEATS OF THE MIGHTY / Gilbert Parker
n76. A SEARCH FOR AMERICA / Frederick Philip Grove
n77. THE BETRAYAL / Henry Kreisel
n78. MAD SHADOWS / Marie-Claire Blais
n79. THE INCOMPARABLE ATUK / Mordecai Richler
n80. THE LUCK OF GINGER COFFEY / Brian Moore
n81. JOHN SUTHERLAND: ESSAYS, CONTROVERSIES AND POEMS / Miriam Waddington
n82. PEACE SHALL DESTROY MANY / Rudy Henry Wiebe
n83. A VOICE FROM THE ATTIC / Robertson Davies
n84. PROCHAIN EPISODE / Hubert Aquin
n85. ROGER SUDDEN / Thomas H. Raddall
n86. MIST ON THE RIVER / Hubert Evans
n87. THE FIRE-DWELLERS / Margaret Laurence
n88. THE DESERTER / Douglas LePan
n89. ANTOINETTE DE MIRECOURT / Rosanna Leprohon
n90. ALLEGRO / Felix Leclerc
n91. THE END OF THE WORLD AND OTHER STORIES / Mavis Gallant
n92. IN THE VILLAGE OF VIGER AND OTHER STORIES / Duncan Campbell Scott
n93. THE EDIBLE WOMAN / Margaret Atwood
n94. IN SEARCH OF MYSELF / Frederick Philip Grove
n95. FEAST OF STEPHEN / Robertson Davies
n96. A BIRD IN THE HOUSE / Margaret Laurence
n97. THE WOODEN SWORD / Edward McCourt
n98. PRIDE'S FANCY / Thomas Raddall
n99. OX BELLS AND FIREFLIES / Ernest Buckler
n100. ABOVE GROUND / Jack Ludwig
n101. NEW PRIEST IN CONCEPTION BAY / Robert Traill Spence Lowell
n102. THE FLYING YEARS / Frederick Niven
n103. WIND WITHOUT RAIN / Selwyn Dewdney
n104. TETE BLANCHE / Marie-Claire Blais

n105. TAY JOHN / Howard O'Hagan
n106. CANADIANS OF OLD / Charles G. D. Roberts
n107. HEADWATERS OF CANADIAN LITERATURE / Andrew MacMechan
n108. THE BLUE MOUNTAINS OF CHINA / Rudy Wiebe
n109. THE HIDDEN MOUNTAIN / Gabrielle Roy
n110. THE HEART OF THE ANCIENT WOOD / Charles G. D. Roberts
n111. JEST OF GOD / Margaret Laurence
n112. SELF CONDEMNED / Wyndham Lewis
n113. DUST OVER THE CITY / André Langevin
n114. OUR DAILY BREAD / Frederick Philip Grove
n115. THE CANADIAN NOVEL IN THE TWENTIETH CENTURY / edited by George Woodcock
n116. THE VIKING HEART / Laura Goodman Salverson
n117. DOWN THE LONG TABLE / Earle Birney
n118. GLENGARRY SCHOOL DAYS / Ralph Connor
n119. THE PLOUFFE FAMILY / Roger Lemelin
n120. WINDFLOWER / Gabrielle Roy
n121. THE DISINHERITED / Matt Cohen
n122. THE TEMPTATIONS OF BIG BEAR / Rudy Wiebe
n123. PANDORA / Sylvia Fraser
n124. HOUSE OF HATE / Percy Janes
n125. A CANDLE TO LIGHT THE SUN / Patricia Blondal
n126. THIS SIDE JORDAN / Margaret Laurence
n127. THE RED FEATHERS / T. G. Roberts
n128. I AM MARY DUNNE / Brian Moore
n129. THE ROAD PAST ALTAMONT / Gabrielle Roy
n130. KNIFE ON THE TABLE / Jacques Godbout
n131. THE MANAWAKA WORLD OF MARGARET LAURENCE / Clara Thomas

o 2. MASKS OF FICTION: CANADIAN CRITICS ON CANADIAN PROSE / edited by A. J. M. Smith
o 3. MASKS OF POETRY: CANADIAN CRITICS ON CANADIAN VERSE / edited by A. J. M. Smith

POETS OF CANADA:

o 1. VOL. I: POETS OF THE CONFEDERATION / edited by Malcolm Ross
o 4. VOL. III: POETRY OF MIDCENTURY / edited by Milton Wilson
o 5. VOL. II: POETS BETWEEN THE WARS / edited by Milton Wilson
o 6. THE POEMS OF EARLE BIRNEY
o 7. VOL. IV: POETS OF CONTEMPORARY CANADA / edited by Eli Mandel
o 8. VOL. V: NINETEENTH-CENTURY NARRATIVE POEMS / edited by David Sinclair
o 9. SELECTED POEMS OF BLISS CARMAN / edited by John Robert Sorfleet
o10. POEMS OF AL PURDY

CANADIAN WRITERS

w 1. MARSHALL MCLUHAN / Dennis Duffy
w 2. E. J. PRATT / Milton Wilson
w 3. MARGARET LAURENCE / Clara Thomas
w 4. FREDERICK PHILIP GROVE / Ronald Sutherland

w 5. LEONARD COHEN / Michael Ondaatje
w 6. MORDECAI RICHLER / George Woodcock
w 7. STEPHEN LEACOCK / Robertson Davis
w 8. HUGH MACLENNAN / Alec Lucas
w 9. EARLE BIRNEY / Richard Robillard
w10. NORTHROP FRYE / Ronald Bates
w11. MALCOLM LOWRY / William H. New
w12. JAMES REANEY / Ross G. Woodman
w13. GEORGE WOODCOCK / Peter Hughes
w14. FARLEY MOWAT / Alec Lucas
w15. ERNEST BUCKLER / Alan Young